The Blame Game

Beverly Sade

ISBN-13: 978-0615990415
ISBN-10: 061599041X

DEDICATION

Tylin Pratt, you're a positive motivating force within my life.
Everything I do is for you. Mommy loves you more than you'll
ever know.

CONTENTS

The Blame Game

A Scandalous Tale

Prologue

As Bonnie sat on the passenger side of her white Range Rover, tears streamed down her angelic face. *This can't be real, this can't be real,* she kept thinking to herself. Bonnie felt as though she was dreaming a terrible dream and she would wake up from this nightmare. She rocked herself back and forth, while holding her stomach, trying to ease the pain that pierced through her entire body.

"Come on Tess, you have to get me there now!" Bonnie screamed at her best friend.

"B calm down, I got you. We're almost there," Tess said, as she tried to maneuver her way through the traffic on highway 76.

Bonnie kept seeing Karl's face and hearing his voice. She thought about everything they'd been through over the years. So much has happened leading up to this dreadful day. They shared many good days and many many bad days, but knowing this could be their last day, hurt Bonnie to the core. Karl was the only man she ever truly loved. Although he had plenty of women, everyone in the streets of Philadelphia knew that only one woman had his heart and that was Bonnie. She was his everything. He only revealed to her who he truly was inside. She knew every part of him. To others Karl was not to be played with and if you're from the streets, that doesn't have to be explained.

"C'mon hun, you ready?" Tess asked, as she rubbed Bonnie on her back.

Bonnie shook her head no and then buried her face in her hands. Tess reached in the backseat and grabbed their pocketbooks. She walked over to the passenger side and helped her best friend out of the car. Bonnie was shaking uncontrollably. Her tight eyes were dazed and blood shot red. Tess held her hand as they walked into the hospital and to the front desk.

"Hello. I'm here to see Karl Atkins," Bonnie said, with her voice trembling.

"Okay give me one moment," the receptionist said. She clicked on her mouse, typed some more and then began to look confused.

"You said Atkins right? A-T-K-I-N-S?" she repeated.

"Yes," Bonnie confirmed.

"I'm sorry sweetie but we don't have a Karl Atkins in the system. When did he come in?" she asked.

"Last night…wait, let me double check," Bonnie replied, as she stepped away.

"Hello Ms. Lynn. Karl is at Penn hospital right?"

"Yes," his mother answered.

"Well, I'm here now and the receptionist is telling me he's not here."

"Bonnie, that's what they've been telling everybody. No one has been able to get in today," she said.

"Well, I'm getting in. Believe that!" Bonnie said, as she walked back over to the receptionist.

"Listen, I have his mom on the phone. She said he's here. She was just here last night. He's in intensive care. Can you just look in the system again please?" Bonnie asked, trying not to show her frustration with the young blonde. The receptionist searched once again and came up with nothing.

"I'm sorry sweetie. I'm still not finding anything," she

said, as she shook her head no.

Another receptionist that was seated at the other end of the desk came over to help. After the blonde explained the situation, she was told to do a search of patients that came in critical condition the night before.

"Here he is, Room 5021. I couldn't find him because he's in the system as unknown," the receptionist said.

"Why is he listed as unknown? Can you add his name now?" Bonnie asked, still holding the cell phone to her ear.

"I'm assuming that when he was brought in, he didn't have proper identification on him. I can't add it now, unless someone is able to provide us with identification."

"Okay, I'll tell his mother to do that. Thank you for your help. How do I get over to ICU?" Bonnie asked.

"Take the escalators to the top level. Make a left at Rhodes hall and take the elevator up to the fifth floor," the receptionist answered.

"Thank you," Bonnie said and then returned back to her phone call.

"Ms. Lynn did you hear what the receptionist was saying about him being listed as unknown?"

"Yes, I heard her. I'll straighten it out today. Are they going to let you see him?" she asked.

"I don't know. I'm on my way up there now. I'll call you and let you know," Bonnie said. She hung up the phone and took a deep breath. Tess grabbed Bonnie's hand, as they walked through the hospital. Bonnie felt like the world was caving in on her. Tess was talking to her and not a single word registered. She was completely out of it. Her feet felt heavy and her legs grew weak. Walking through Rhodes hallway felt like the longest walk she'd ever taken. On the elevator, Bonnie broke down when the number five lit up on the panel. She cried so hard that Tess eyes began to water too. They walked closely together and Tess kept her arms wrapped around Bonnie's shoulders. Once in the intensive care unit, it didn't take them long to find Karl's room. His room was the first on the right. The door was wide open and the curtain was completely pulled back. Bonnie rushed in and saw him lying there all alone.

"Excuse me are you two family?" the nurse asked, as if no one other than family would be allowed in to see him.

"I'm his ex-wife," Bonnie responded, still walking over to Karl's bed.

"Okay. I'll leave you guys alone," the nurse said. Tears began to flow so heavily from Bonnie's eyes.

"Karl. It's me Bonnie. I love you, Karl. Do you hear me? I still love you. I never stopped. Please show me that you can hear me. I'm right here by your side." She grabbed Karl's hand and it felt warm. His head was wrapped with bandages, there were tubes in his mouth and he was connected to a ventilator. Bonnie squeezed his hand tight and placed her left hand on his chest. She felt his chest move up and down and his heart still beating. It looked as though he was only sleeping. Although Bonnie knew he wasn't going to make it, feeling his heart still beating gave her false hope. Bonnie turned to her best friend and started venting.

"Tess, why the hell is he in here all alone? Where is that bitch?" Bonnie said, rolling her neck and pointing her finger.

"I was thinking the same thing but maybe it's because he's listed as unknown," Tess responded.

"We got in didn't we? She didn't try very hard then. I thought I was gonna walk in here and see her by his side." Bonnie grabbed her cell phone and called Karl's mother again.

"Did you get in Bonnie?" his mother said, anxiously.

"Yup I sure did and why is he here all by himself? Didn't he marry that chick? Why is she not by her husband's side?" Bonnie questioned.

"She told me that she's taking it hard and she can't see him like that."

"What! That's bullshit. I'm sorry, excuse my language but that makes no sense to me. You think I want to see him like this? But I'm here, because my heart won't let me do anything but be here." At this point, Bonnie's emotions were all over the place. She was angry and hurt at the same time. She knew how much Karl hated being alone. He didn't even like to sleep alone and there he was lying on his deathbed all by himself.

"I know Bonnie. I know. You're there with him aren't you? You're right there by his side…and that's how he would've wanted it to be," Ms. Lynn said, trying to calm Bonnie down.

"Ms. Lynn, I think there's a chance he'll come out of this. When I was talking to him the machine kept going off. I know that he can hear me. I just know he can. Karl is strong. He's gonna pull through," Bonnie said, with tears rolling down her face.

"No, sweetheart. He's not. The only thing keeping him alive right now is that machine. He's been declared brain dead. Do you understand what that means?" his mother said, in a very low and disgruntled voice.

"No, not really," she replied. Bonnie understood exactly what she was being told but she just couldn't fathom it.

"You don't want to understand it. Bonnie I know how much you love my son. And he loved you. I knew that if anyone was going to get in to see Karl, it would be you. Don't cry baby. You have so many memories… cherish them all, even the bad ones. You hear?" Ms. Lynn said, barely able to finish her sentences.

"Yes. I hear you. My heart hurts so bad right now. I just…I don't know. I'm gonna let you go. I'm staying here for a while. I'll call you later," Bonnie replied.

"Okay sweetheart. Be strong. I love you."

"I love you too Ms. Lynn. Bye."

Although it was extremely hard for Bonnie to see Karl in this state, she knew she didn't want to leave him. She told Tess she wanted to stay with him for a while. Tess told Bonnie she would take her car and come back to get her whenever she felt ready. Bonnie walked over to the huge window in Karl's room. She stared out and her mind began to drift. Her thoughts of what she and Karl shared were interrupted when a red headed nurse entered the room.

"Hello. I'll be his nurse for the rest of the evening. Are you his wife?" she asked.

"Ex-wife. Can I ask you a question?"

"Sure," she said, with a pleasant smile on her face.

"Isn't there a chance that he'll pull through? I know everyone is saying that he's brain dead, but why is he sweating? Why is it that every time I talk to him, the machine starts beeping? Does that mean that his vital signs are going up?" she quizzed.

The pitiful look in Bonnie's eyes made it difficult for the nurse to speak the truth. She took a deep breath before she answered her questions.

"In his case, no. His injuries are so severe that, we're certain he won't make it. The doctors ran several test and he didn't respond to any of them. Even though his brain stem and his lungs are no longer functioning, the heart continues to beat because it's artificially being supplied oxygen from the ventilator. His heart will only continue to beat for a short amount of time. In most cases, two to three days," she said.

"But…what about the machine beeping? When I…" Before Bonnie could even finish her sentence the nurse cut her off.

"Sometimes the machine just does that. It doesn't mean that he's responding at all. It has nothing to do with him," she replied.

The nurse positioned the suction tube in Karl's mouth to catch his drool. She then apologized to Bonnie and gently patted her on her right shoulder, before leaving the room. Bonnie pulled a chair close to Karl's bed. She then grabbed his hand and kissed it.

"I don't care what they say baby. I know you can hear me. I love you. You have to know that right? It's always been you and me Karl. We've been through so much together. This is not how it's supposed to end. You said you'll never leave me…remember? Don't you remember saying that?" Bonnie felt in her heart that Karl could hear every word she was saying. She held his hand tight and began to reminisce. Reminisce on their love and how it all began...

Chapter One
Graduation: Class of 2002

Bonnie, Tess, and Monique sat at the dinner table like three make pretend Charlie's angels. They plotted out their future and decided as a team, what their next move should be. These girls were joined at the hip ever since freshman year of high school and couldn't imagine life being any different. Each of them were drop dead gorgeous and although they had different personalities, they meshed very well together. Tess was slim and stood about 5'10. She had beautiful, chocolate skin, wide, light-brown eyes and was told on a regular basis she looked like Taral Hicks from the movie, "Belly." Everybody loved them some Tess. She didn't like drama and tried her hardest to stay away from it but don't get it twisted, Tess was no punk. She gave out a fair share of beat downs around the way and because of it nobody tried her. Monique was 5'7, light skinned, curvy, and kept her hair cut short like Kelis and dyed blonde like Beyonce'. The girls loved to hate Monique. She was sassy and didn't take shit from anyone. She was a bit of a firecracker and was always ready to pop off. Then, there was Bonnie. Bonnie was 5'6, and very curvy. She had tight, almond shaped eyes, beautiful caramel skin that was smooth as butter, and full pink lips. Bonnie's long, dark hair matched perfectly with her dark eyebrows and long, dark eyelashes. In addition to her good looks, she was also very intelligent. While her two best friends barely made it through school, she graduated with honors and actually looked forward to attending college. Tess and Monique, however, had other plans.

"I'm so glad we're finally out of that hellhole!" Monique said, enthusiastically.

"Girl that makes two of us. So, what are we going to do now? What's next for us?" Tess asked.

"I'm going to Drexel. It's not too late for ya'll to apply. Maybe ya'll can even go to Community College for a semester and then transfer," Bonnie said. She couldn't imagine college life without her girls.

"Well that's not happening. You know I love you Bonnie, but I hate school with a passion. There has to be another way for me. Shit, cause I can't do school all over again," Monique said, while picking over her plate of Chicken & Shrimp Alfredo.

"Cosign!" Tess said, and then snapped her fingers. All three of them burst into laughter.

"No, but seriously Bonnie. Being a college girl is you all the way. You're so smart and I know you're going to do great things with your life. You have to go. Besides, your dad is not going to have it any other way," Tess added.

"She's right," Monique said.

"But I need ya'll there with me. It's always been us three," Bonnie said, trying to put on her sad puppy dog face.

"Just because we're not going to school together, doesn't mean that our friendship will change. Stop worrying about nothing. Everything is gonna be just fine," Tess said, in a very soothing voice.

"Yeah girl stop tripping! I mean damn, look at us. We're young, we look good…hell, we're about to find out what life is all about," Monique said, slapping Tess's hand.

"Okay! I'm tryna pull me a player. Better yet, we all need a player," Tess said.

"Ya'll crazy," Bonnie said, while laughing. "I'm not thinking about no players right now. I'm just tryna get me a little job and stay focused, so I can get through school."

"Well listen, school doesn't start up for another three

months. We have to be out here for the summer. We need to be at these parties ya'll," Monique said.

"You know I'm down but somebody please tell me how our little eighteen-year old asses is gonna get into these parties," Bonnie said.

"Easy. We'll get fake IDs. I already know a guy that does it," Monique replied.

"Monique your ass is always into something," Bonnie teased, and then all the girls laughed out loud.

The bond they shared was one between blood sisters. They genuinely had a deep love for one another. Tess came from a good family. She was raised in the church and her parents instilled good values in her as a child. Her parents were still going strong after fifteen years of marriage. She had four older brothers, which explained her rough, tomboy side. She always yearned for that sisterly love, so clicking with Monique and Bonnie was something special to her.

Monique and Bonnie were both raised by their fathers. Monique's mother battled with a drug addiction for many years. After she gave birth, doctors ran test and found crack cocaine in Monique's system. Child Protective Services immediately stepped in and placed her in foster care. For Monique's father, this was the last straw. Monique's mother had everyone fooled. She'd been lying and telling them that she was clean for over a year. Her father tried with everything inside of him to help her. No matter how many times he sent her to rehab, she would eventually relapse. Although he loved her, he couldn't let a stranger raise his daughter. So, he got custody of Monique and left her mother for good. That still wasn't enough to keep her clean and she remained absent from Monique's life.

Bonnie didn't move with her father until the age of thirteen. She was raised in Athens, Georgia by her mother Karen Summers. This is who Bonnie inherited her enticing looks from. Karen was a piece of work. She was known as one of the most cut-throat, gold digging whores in the state of Georgia. She dealt with ball players, drug dealers, judges and even preachers. Whoever had enough money for her to dig into. Karen provided Bonnie with a very lavish lifestyle but was uninvolved as a parent. Bonnie was practically raising herself, while her mother was busy juggling all of her men. When Bonnie was about twelve years old her mother met a drug dealer, named Chase. He was the worst kind of man. The kind of man with absolutely no respect for women. They were only dating two weeks, when Karen moved him into her home. He didn't waste any time showing his true colors either. He beat Karen unconscious once, in front of Bonnie. Karen promised her daughter she wouldn't take him back and that things would go back to how it was before, when it was just the two of them. Many nights Bonnie would climb into bed with her mother and run her fingers through her hair, trying to console her after those horrendous fights she would have with Chase.

"Why do you let him do this to you? He's trying to break you down and he's winning. Don't you want to be happy again mommy?" Bonnie asked.

"I am happy baby. We're just going through a tough time but he loves me. He loves both of us," Karen said, lying to herself.

"He doesn't love us. He doesn't even know us mommy. What makes him think he can come into our lives and destroy it? He's not going to change…he's only going to get worse."

Bonnie was right. She watched their lives spiral out of control. A year passed, and Chase continued to abuse Karen, mentally and physically. By this time Bonnie had enough. She called her father, Michael and told him that she was finally ready to live with him. He'd been wanting Bonnie in Philly with him for the longest but she didn't want to leave her mother. Although she wasn't the greatest mother and she made many mistakes, Bonnie loved her deeply. She knew Chase had a hold on her, something terrible. And in her heart, she knew the best thing for her to do was to leave. She would rather do that, than to have it ruin their relationship. Bonnie was mature like that. At twelve years old, Bonnie understood a lot about life. People would always tell her she'd been here before. Her aunts and older cousins who were in their thirties would call Bonnie for relationship advice and even ask her to write love letters for them. She was a deep young girl with an old soul.

Now that Bonnie was out of high school, she wanted to find herself a job. She didn't want something that would require a lot of work. She didn't need a job that would stress her out, especially since she would be attending college in the fall. She decided to go downtown and search for a job in retail. It was easy for the young, pretty girls to get hired at the men's clothing stores. She walked into City Blue and five minutes later left with a job. She didn't have to fill out an application or anything. A heavy-set Israeli guy looked her up and down and hired her on the spot. He told her that she could start the following day. It was just that easy and Bonnie was ecstatic about it. Everything was falling into place. Bonnie worked from nine-to-five, five days a week. She loved her new job. She worked at one of the most popular, urban stores in the city. It was a fun and exciting environment and she met all kinds of people. On top of it all, she was getting paid cash weekly.

One day, Bonnie took her thirty minute lunch break and went to Dunkin Donuts, around the corner from her job. While she was waiting in line a handsome Israeli man approached her.

"Hi, I'm Shai. Do you work around here?"

"Yeah, I work around the corner at City Blue," Bonnie said.

"City Blue? You're too pretty to be working at City Blue. Who are you working for, Mike?" Shai said, with a devilish grin on his face.

"Yeah. You don't like him?" Bonnie asked.

"No. He's trash. How much is he paying you over there?"

"Seven dollars an hour. Why?"

"I want you to come work for me, at the Net. I'll pay

you nine dollars an hour, plus you get commission," he said. Shai gave Bonnie an offer she couldn't refuse.

"Deal. When can I start?"

"You can start tomorrow if you'd like," he replied.

"I don't want to just quit on him like that. I'll finish out the week and start on Monday if that's okay with you," she said. "My name is Bonnie by the way."

"Okay. I'll see you on Monday Bonnie. Be there at 9:30. My store is at 1901 Chestnut St."

"Thanks Shai. I'll see you then!" Bonnie said, with a huge smile on her face.

Bonnie couldn't wait to start her new job. She finished out the rest of the week at City Blue and to her surprise, Mike wasn't upset about her leaving. He told her that if things didn't work out at the Net, she could always come back to work for him. Bonnie couldn't be any happier with how things were turning out. All of her plans were coming together. She was making her own money and becoming more independent. Ever since she moved to Philadelphia, her father kept her on a short leash. And she was definitely a daddy's girl. He did everything for her. He washed her clothes, cooked for her, cleaned her room and drove her any and everywhere she needed to go. Now that she was grown and out of high school he was finally letting up. Bonnie was overjoyed by this newfound freedom.

At the Net, everything was on another level. It was definitely a step up from City Blue. The store was huge. There was a dramatic entrance, upstairs and downstairs, a classic, curved staircase and Brazilian hardwood floors. At City Blue, Bonnie was used to selling Rocawear, Akademic, Girbaud, Sean John and Enyce clothing. Here she would be selling Diesel, Prada, Gucci, Christian Dior and Louis Vuitton. A lot of rappers, athletes, and street guys with money shopped at the Net. There were five locations throughout Philly but none of them popped the way this one did. Yes, they had all of the hottest designer clothing, but they were also known for having some of the prettiest girls working in their stores. Shai knew the guys would love Bonnie and that she would bring a lot of attention to the store. He introduced her to the rest of the girls as his lucky charm and they were sick about it. Something about her made them feel uneasy. Maybe it was the fact that she was much younger than them or the fact that they knew the customers would go crazy over her. Whatever it was they just didn't like her and Bonnie could care less.

After only a month, Bonnie was the top seller at the Net. She didn't have to try hard because all of the guys approached her first. Most of the time, they already knew what they wanted to buy anyway. She would just follow them around the store, while they flirted with her. Occasionally, she would flirt back. Especially, if they were spending a lot of money. That would only make her commission check even fatter. There were all kinds of guys trying to get with Bonnie. The type of guys that Monique and Tess were on the prowl for. Although Bonnie hadn't met anyone she was really into, she always took their numbers and made them take her and the girls out on triple dates. It seemed like every other night they were out on a date, with different players. They were beginning to see Philly in a whole new light.

None of the girls had their own car and Tess was tired of borrowing her mother's car and being hassled about when to bring it back. Bonnie decided it was time to get her own. She and her two best friends caught the train to Broad and Wyoming, to check out a used car lot she found listed in the newspaper. She only had about eight hundred dollars to spend. The salesman showed her a 1989, silver Chrysler Sebring coupe. It wasn't her dream car but it would definitely serve its purpose. She needed something to get around in. Besides, she just got her license and wasn't the best driver. This was the perfect little car to run around in and improve her driving skills. He sold the car to her for only five hundred dollars. She spent another two hundred dollars on tags and registration. Bonnie, Monique and Tess drove right off the lot and all around Philly. You would've thought they were in a brand new Mercedes, the way they were smiling from ear to ear with the top dropped. They couldn't wait to get down South Street.

South Street was one of the most popular hangout spots. It was filled with clubs, bars, restaurants, and tons of shops. It was similar to Canal Street in New Orleans. Their first stop was Ishkabibbles. They had the best Philly cheese steaks ever. The girls placed their orders and then sat down and waited for their food.

"Monique, what's up with those fake IDs? We need those like ASAP!" Bonnie said.

"I talked to him. He told me to send him pictures of us and he'll steal IDs from the strippers he thinks resemble us," Monique replied.

"What! That's too much," Bonnie said. "His ass is gon' get fired. Why can't we just get fake IDs with our picture on it?"

"We were but he said that nowadays the security at the clubs scan them to make sure they're real."

"Well, I don't need one. My cousin Tasha said I can use hers anytime and ya'll know we look just alike," Tess butted in.

"Yeah, ya'll sure do." Monique said. "So, I'll tell him to hook me and Bonnie up then."

"Next Thursday, Dipset will be at Chrome. We're in there for sure!" Bonnie said, with excitement.

"Oh, you already know!" Monique said, while slapping Bonnie's hand.

After eating and window shopping, Bonnie dropped her girlfriends off and then went home to prepare for the next day. She had to be at work at nine the following morning. Her father was upset about her going out and buying a car without discussing it with him first. Bonnie didn't have the energy to argue with her father over what she did with her own money. She brushed him off and said they would talk about it later. After Bonnie got out of the shower, she climbed into bed and reached under her mattress to get her journal. She wrote in her journal daily and began every entry with Dear God. She'd been writing Dear God letters ever since she was a little girl.

Dear God,

    I just want to thank you for bringing so much good into my life. Everything seems to be falling into place for me and I know it's all because of you. Please continue to keep me on the right track God and bless my friends and family as well. Can you look out for my mother. I don't think she's happy and I worry about her a lot. I wish she was here with me. Please bring positive changes into her life and help her to find happiness within. That's it for now. Amen.

    Monique's friend came through with the IDs just like he promised. Monique, Tess and Bonnie were so excited about going to the party at Chrome Nightclub. Tess had a thing for Juelz Santana. She thought he was so sexy and she was ready to go all out for him that night. The girls drove to King of Prussia mall and did some shopping, then went to get their hair, nails and feet done. They all went to Monique's house to get ready. Monique's hair was freshly dyed blonde, and cut short. She wore a tight fitted, black dress with the entire back cut out. Tess had a long wet and wavy weave, with a part down the middle. She wore a studded bra, and high waist pants. Bonnie pulled her hair back in a bun and put on one hell of a freakum dress. It was a royal blue, lace dress with a low cut neckline, that made her cleavage sit up nicely.

    When they arrived at Chrome, the line was down the block. This made them even more excited. They put the last touches on their makeup and made sure their hair was intact, then they joined everyone else in line. Bonnie and Monique were a little nervous about their IDs. They were praying and hoping they wouldn't be turned away, and have to take the walk of shame. Tess wasn't the least bit worried. She and her cousin could pass for twins. They waited for at least twenty minutes, before they reached the front of the line. The bouncers thoroughly checked their pocketbooks but barely even looked at their IDs. They were too concentrated on how good their bodies looked in those tight, and revealing clothes.

"Thanks to Bonnie and that big ol' butt, he wasn't paying our IDs no mind," Monique said, laughing.

"I know right and look at this joint. It's popping up in here!" Tess said, while switching extra hard.

"Come on ya'll, let's get some drinks," Bonnie said.

The club was packed from wall to wall. All eyes were on them, as they made their way through the crowd. Guys were grabbing and pulling on them left and right. The girls ordered three vodka and cranberry drinks, and then posted up against the wall, to scope the scene. The diplomats performed their hit song, "Dipset Anthem" and the crowd went nuts. The girls danced sexy, and seductively, while sipping on their drinks.

"Excuse me. Can I talk to you for a minute?" This man was fine as hell. He had dark skin, a low haircut, a nicely groomed beard, and sparkling white teeth. He stood about 6'2 and had crazy swag.

"Sure," Bonnie replied.

"I just have to tell you that you're so pretty," he said. "What's your name?"

"Thank You. My name is Bonnie."

"I'm Karl. I would love to take you out sometime. Will you let me?"

"No, I'm sorry. I have a boyfriend," Bonnie said.

"Well, can we just be friends?" Karl replied, knowing that he wanted to be more than just friends.

"No, I don't do that. I'm a good girl. I'm faithful to my man," she said, while smiling at him.

"Damn. I gotta respect that. I won't bother you. Enjoy the rest of your night alright," he said.

Karl looked very disappointed. Bonnie knew he wanted her badly. She could also tell he was the type of man that was used to getting anything he wanted, including any girl. Karl walked back over to his homeboy, but didn't go too far. He purposely kept Bonnie in his sight.

"What she say man?" Karl's friend asked.

"Shorty said she got a man," he replied.

"So what."

"Trust me playa. I tried," Karl said. "She bad as shit nigga."

The minute Karl walked away Tess and Monique were checking Bonnie, for not giving him her number. Monique especially couldn't believe that Bonnie wasn't feeling him. All Monique saw when she looked at him was dollar signs.

"Bonnie, are you crazy? Did you see all that damn ice around his neck and wrist?" Monique said. Tess immediately chimed in and agreed with Monique.

It was evident that Karl was doing very well for himself and any fool could see he wasn't your average nine-to-five working, do good type either. Truth be told, Karl was one of the biggest drug dealers in the city of Philadelphia. His life of crime began at the tender age of fourteen. He was introduced to the game by his old head, Blanco. Blanco was a ruthless killer and a drug dealer. In the beginning, all Karl did was look after Blanco's Pit Bulls. He would go over to Blanco's house every day after school to walk, feed and clean up after them. Even though Karl was just a kid, Blanco considered him one of his closest friends. He trusted him with everything...all of his secrets and all of his money. When Karl was seventeen, Blanco was indicted on murder and drug charges. He was sentenced to life, plus 50 years in prison. The FEDS found 300,000 in cash, 12 guns, and 350 grams of cocaine in his half a million dollar home, in Huntington Valley. There was another small stash, buried in the backyard and only Karl knew where to find it. Karl took the 50,000 that he found, and everything that he learned from Blanco, and began his career as a street hustler.

At the age of twenty one Karl was sent to prison to serve a ten year sentence for a murder. He was released two years early but he violated his parole and was sent back to prison for a year. This time he'd been out of prison for only eighteen months. Although Karl hated prison, he returned back to the same lifestyle each and every time. He just couldn't get out…no matter how hard he tried.

Bonnie heard her girlfriends loud and clear but she wasn't impressed with all of that nonsense. She didn't care about how much money he could potentially have. She looked for much more in a man. Besides, she was trying to stay focused, stick to her plans and avoid any distractions. And by looking at Karl, she could tell that he was one big distraction.

"Yes, I seen his neck and wrist. So what," Bonnie said, to Monique.

"Girl stop tripping, you need to go talk to him," Monique said.

"She's right Bonnie. Look at him. He looks sooo good," Tess added, while peeking over at him.

"Well, I already told him I have a boyfriend. I'm gonna look stupid if I go over there," she said.

After being pumped up tremendously by her girls, Bonnie motioned for Karl to come to her. She watched him closely that night and seeing him turn down every girl that approached him turned her on. Karl walked over to Bonnie with the biggest smile on his face. He just knew he would get her number this time.

"Hey," Bonnie said.

"What's up beautiful?"

"I've changed my mind. You can take my number."

"What about your man, that you're so true to?" he asked, sarcastically.

"I don't have a man. I turned you down, because I wanted to see if you would just move on to the next chick," Bonnie said, lying through her teeth. She couldn't tell him that her girlfriends persuaded her into talking to him.

"Oh so you put me through a lil' test huh?" He laughed. "Shit, well I guess I passed."

"You definitely passed baby," she said, smiling.

She gave him the sweetest look and Karl was mesmerized by her beauty. They talked briefly, and then exchanged numbers. Nelly's "Hot in Herre" came on and everyone became hype instantly. Tess and Monique rushed back over and pulled Bonnie onto the dance floor. They knew this was her song and they wanted her to show Karl what she was working with. "Break that shit down Bonnie!" Monique yelled, as Bonnie rolled her hips and popped her ass. She moved her body in a circular motion and dropped down to the floor, only to come back up seductively, with her ass poked out. Tess and Monique started doing the Beyoncé's booty pop and the three of them were the center of attention. Karl couldn't take his eyes off of Bonnie, while she was on the dance floor. He knew right then and there she would be his girl.

The let out was like another party all over again. Range Rovers, Escalades, BMW's and other expensive cars were parked with music blasting. Girls were still dancing and acting a fool in the street. People loved the let outs for many reasons. The main reason was it gave you a chance to see what he or she really looked like for real and not under the nightclub lighting. Another reason was that the people who didn't actually go to the party, could still come through to see who wore what and who did what. Bonnie, Tess and Monique weren't interested in hanging around with everyone else. They felt like they were too decent to play anybody's let out.

Bonnie dropped Tess and Monique off and then headed home. Just as she pulled up in front of her house, her cell phone started ringing. It was an unfamiliar number and she knew that only one person could be calling her at 2:30 in the morning. Who else other than Karl would've known she was still up.

"Hello," Bonnie answered.

"Hey Pretty. It's Karl," he said. "What you doing?"

"Nothing, just pulling up in front of my house."

"Let's go get something to eat. You hungry?"

"No, not really. I'm tired," she said, while getting out of the car.

"Well can I come see you?" he asked.

The first thing that ran through Bonnie's mind was that he was trying to get some. Why else would he be trying to come over at this time. *Hell, these are booty call hours,* she thought to herself.

"Umm I don't think that's such a good idea," she said.

"Listen Bonnie, I don't have to come in. We can sit in the car if you want. I just want to see you." Karl didn't have any intentions on sleeping with her that night. He just wanted to be around her.

"Okay. Come on. I live right off of Broad and Lindley, on the corner of 16th street. Call me when you're outside."

"Ok. I'll be right there baby."

Bonnie hurried inside and upstairs to her room. Her father was sound asleep. Even though she was grown, she knew that her father wouldn't be too pleased about a guy like Karl coming by the house. She slipped out of her clothes and put on a tank top and a pair of thin sweat pants. She washed all of the makeup off her face and pulled her hair to the top of her head in a bun. She called her best friends to let them know she made it home safely and of course she had to tell them that Karl was on his way to see her.

It didn't take Karl long to arrive at Bonnie's house. He called her and told her to come downstairs. She peeked out of the window and saw that he was driving a black 2002 Mercedes Benz CLS, with Asanti custom luxury rims. She checked the mirror once again, before leaving out of the house. She wanted to look chill, like she wasn't trying too hard but still cute at the same time.

Bonnie and Karl sat outside on the front steps. He couldn't believe how good she looked. She looked even better to him without all the makeup and tight clothes.

"So, who do you live here with?" he asked.

"My dad."

"Oh yeah. So, you from up this way?"

"Kinda sorta. I lived in Atlanta with my mom, up until I was thirteen and then I came here with my dad," she said.

"What about you? Where you from?"

"I'm from West Philly, down the bottom. Born and raised," he said.

Karl wondered to himself why she left Atlanta, and had to move with her dad but he didn't want to pry. It was too soon for all of that.

"How old are you?" Bonnie asked.

"I'm thirty-three."

"Yeah right. No you're not!" she said.

"I'm dead serious. How old do I look?"

"Like twenty six, twenty seven."

"I get that a lot. How old are you?" he asked.

"Eighteen."

"Get the fuck outta here. You're not eighteen yo."

"I swear," she said, while laughing.

"How did you get in Chrome?"

"I used someone else's ID." They both started laughing. Here it was, she was thinking he was younger and he was thinking that she was older.

"You don't carry yourself like a eighteen year old. You're very mature for your age. I like that...I like that a lot," he said.

They sat out there on the steps and talked... and talked. Although there was a huge age difference, they had a lot in common. They both loved to write and even shared the same taste in music. Every song he threw at Bonnie, she knew it and would start singing the lyrics. He told her that she had an old soul and that he never met anyone her age who listened to "Minnie Ripperton, Angela Bofill, Atlantic Starr, and Norman Conners. He liked Bonnie being on his level mentally. He too was a deep conversationalist. He wasn't your average street guy. He was very intelligent and book smart. Bonnie was intrigued by him and she wanted to get into his world. She loved everything about him. She never felt such a strong connection with anyone else. There was no denying the chemistry between the two. Karl hadn't sat on the steps like this and talked for hours with any woman. With

Bonnie, it was just different. He really wanted to get to know her. Three o' clock, turned into four, four turned into five, five turned into six and they were still on the steps talking. Bonnie told him repeatedly to go home and he didn't want to leave. He wanted to stay with her. She could tell that he was getting sleepy, because he kept nodding off. It was seven o' clock in the morning, when he finally decided to leave. They both stood up and hugged each other, as if they'd been long time lovers. He kissed her on the forehead and told her that he would see her later.

"I don't even want to leave you," he said. "I don't want you to go either," she replied. Them not wanting to leave each other that night would mark the beginning of a crazy and ongoing love affair.

CHAPTER TWO
Crazy in Love

It was Tess's cousin's wedding day and she invited the girls. Bonnie told Karl that she wanted him to come along as her date. It would be Bonnie's first time at a wedding and she wanted to experience that moment with him. It had only been three days since they met and they were inseparable. He wanted her right next to him, no matter what he was doing. Whether he was running the streets handling business, making drop offs, or collecting his money, he wanted Bonnie on the passenger side. He bragged to everyone that he had the prettiest young girl in the city. Karl was in love with her beauty and even more in love with her being so young. He didn't have to worry about her being ran through by other guys around the way, or showing her picture to someone and hearing them say "Oh yeah, I fucked her." In his eyes, she was untainted. She was Philly's best kept secret and Karl would be the one to introduce her…but as his chick.

Bonnie and Karl arrived at the wedding dressed to impress. Karl was wearing a black linen short set, with a pair of classic Gucci lug sole moccasins. Bonnie wore a black and white polka dot Chanel dress, a pair of red six inch Gucci stilettos, and she carried a red Chanel clutch, that brought out her shoes. Karl bought her entire outfit. He had every intention on showing up to shut it down. That's just how he was. He was a flashy guy, that loved for all eyes to be on him. When they walked through the door people definitely took notice. Bonnie's walk alone made both men and women stare. She had a killer walk ever since she was a little girl. If you didn't know her, you would've thought she was intentionally putting this walk on for show but it was natural. Karl told Bonnie to wear her hair out for him, being as though he only seen it pulled back in a bun. She had a deep part in the middle and it was pressed out bone straight. Her hair hung long, past her shoulders. She had on very little makeup. Just a little eyeliner, mascara and lip gloss. She looked absolutely gorgeous.

During the ceremony, Bonnie held Karl's hand tight and they exchanged more than a few smiles at one another. It was something about that moment that made Bonnie feel that much closer to him and vice versa. He whispered in her ear, "I love you B." She looked at him and without hesitation replied, "I love you too." As crazy as it seemed, they didn't doubt for one second that it was real. It didn't matter that they only knew each other for three days. Karl had never felt this way before and neither had she. So they were ready to dive in head first.

The reception was held at a hood spot in West Philly. They had a good ol' time too. Karl, Bonnie, Tess and Monique all sat at a table together. They finally had the chance to get to know the guy who their girl was so crazy about. Karl had a great sense of humor and he and Bonnie together were two comedians. They laughed and cracked jokes about almost everyone there. Karl whispered in Bonnie's ear, "Baby what kind of champagne is this? It ain't even bubbly." She just laughed and shook her head. Monique and Tess thought they were perfect for each other. When the DJ played, Mr. Cheeks "Lights, Camera, Action" Bonnie jumped up from the table and said, "Oh shit ya'll this our song!" Tess and Monique were ready as always. Bonnie grabbed Karl's hand and pulled him onto the dance floor. She turned her back towards him and started popping her ass on him. He just stood there proud, nodding his head to the music with a look on his face like *Yeah that's my bitch.*

All of the thirsty West Philly hoochies were in the building that day. And one of them tried to push up on Karl, right in front of Bonnie. While they were on the dance floor, a light skinned chick with hair weaved all down her back, tapped him on the shoulder and asked him if he wanted to dance. He shut her down of course and before she could walk away, Bonnie turned to her and said, "He with me. Get your thirsty ass out of here!" After seeing the look on Bonnie's face, she didn't want any trouble. Karl wrapped his arms around her and said, "Yo, you crazy. You gon' be my wife you know dat." They laughed and hugged each other tight.

After they left the reception Karl took Bonnie to his mother's house. She lived in West Philly, right off of 52nd and Parkside. Bonnie had no idea whose house they were going to until, he turned the key in the lock.

"Who house is this? Bonnie asked.

"My moms."

"Karl, I don't want to meet your mom like this," she said, looking down at her short, tight fitting dress.

"My mom cool. She don't care about that," he said.

Bonnie was still nervous. She knew how much he loved his mom, and she wanted to make a good impression. All of the nervousness quickly vanished, when seen how cool Ms. Lynn was. She gave her the biggest hug and said, "So this is who I've been hearing so much about." They all sat in the living room for a good hour and just talked. Karl and his mother had a strong bond. He talked to her as if she was one of his homeys. It wasn't disrespectful in any kind of way. He was just very open with her and Bonnie admired that about their relationship. When they were leaving out his mother made a joke about Bonnie being so young and that she didn't have any miles on her. She told Bonnie that she could give her a lot of grandbabies. They all laughed and Karl said, "Oh yeah, we got you on that!"

Now that Bonnie had officially met his mother, she wanted to introduce him to her father. Michael wouldn't be as warm and inviting as Ms. Lynn. He didn't think anyone was good enough to date his daughter. When Karl drove Bonnie back to her house, she called her father and told him to come outside. She and Karl got out of the car, she looked him up and down and then quickly told him to tuck his diamond K necklace in his shirt. She knew that him seeing the brand new Mercedes Benz would already have his mind wondering. From the moment he saw Karl he immediately didn't like him for his daughter. He could tell that he was much older than her. On top of that, he knew that he was into the streets and he just got a bad vibe from him.

"Daddy, I want you to meet Karl."

"Hello Sir. Nice to meet you," he said, while shaking Michael's hand.

"Nice to meet you as well," he said.

There was an awkward silence. Bonnie could tell that her dad wasn't feeling Karl, so she hugged him and said that she would call him later. The minute they got inside the house, he started interrogating her.

"Bonnie, what are you doing with him? Where did you even meet a guy like that?"

"What do you mean a guy like that? Daddy he's a really good guy," Bonnie said.

"There is nothing good about him. I'm telling you, all I see is trouble. I hope you're not actually taking him serious," Michael said, using a firm voice.

"You haven't even given him a chance. You were around him for less than three minutes and you think you have him all figured out," she fired back.

"I'm your father Bonnie. That's all it takes for me to know if someone is right for my daughter or not. I know you think you're grown now and you want to make your own decisions. That's fine. But I don't approve of him. And I don't want him to ever step foot in this house. You understand?"

"Whatever," Bonnie said, as she walked off and stormed upstairs like a fifth grader. She wasn't trying to hear anything her father was saying. Bonnie was very headstrong and once she made her mind up about something there wasn't anything that anyone could do to change it.

Over the next few weeks, Karl picked Bonnie up from work every day. She'd been spending all of her time with him. By this time, she'd met his children, twelve year old Karl Junior, and eleven year old Sierra. His son was a splitting image of him. His daughter was a beautiful, chocolate girl. She was tall and slim, just like her father. Bonnie stayed at Karl's house so much, that she kept most of her things there. He had plenty of female friends before meeting Bonnie. It seemed as if he was with a different woman every other day. And now things were different.

One day Karl's phone kept ringing, but he wouldn't answer it. Bonnie knew that it had to be a woman calling him like that. She made him answer the phone and put it on speaker.

"Yo!" he answered.

"What do you mean, yo! Why haven't you been answering my calls?" the woman said.

"I've been busy," Karl said.

"Tell her you got a girl now and not to call you no more," Bonnie, said while rolling her eyes.

The woman heard Bonnie on the other end of the phone. "Who is that?" she asked.

"That's my girl."

"Your girl? When did you get a girl?" she asked.

"It doesn't matter. That's my girl. Don't call me no more alright." Karl just hung up the phone.

"Who was that?" Bonnie asked.

"Vicky. She's nobody…just an old friend," he said.

They laid in bed together and she wrapped her legs around him. Karl wanted Bonnie for a while now. Even though they were only together for a month, Karl was tired of waiting, especially since he was putting time in with her every day. Bonnie had intentions on making him wait at least three months. It was actually her two best friends that told her repeatedly, "If you don't make a man wait, he'll put you in the same category as all the other chicks." Bonnie was over all that nonsense at this point and was ready to give herself to him. She climbed on top of him, looked deeply into his eyes and kissed him intensely. He grabbed her ass and instantly became hard as a rock. He opened his dresser drawer and reached for a Trojan. When Bonnie saw how big he was, she was thinking *Oh shit he's gonna kill my ass.* She had only been with one other guy before him and he was nowhere as big as Karl. It had been almost a year since she had sex but after he warmed her body up, she was ready for whatever. Karl wasn't the love making type of guy. He didn't even like to go down on a woman but the way he went down on Bonnie that night, you would've thought it was his most favorite thing to do. He was into rough, dirty sex. Something that Bonnie knew nothing about. He had to tell her how he liked to be fucked and sucked. He taught her how to get nasty and she was on point with everything. And from that moment, she had him hooked.

The next day, the both of them carried on like two impulsive teenagers. Karl told Bonnie that she should get his name tattooed on her. He didn't mention anything about him doing the same. So, Bonnie immediately checked him. "Yeah, we should go get tattoos," she said, while rolling her neck. He replied, "Let's do it then." Without hesitation, they went to a tattoo parlor on South Street. Bonnie got Karl tattooed on her lower back and he got Bonnie tattooed on his upper left arm. This was their foolish way of letting everyone know that they belonged to each other, and Karl wouldn't take her belonging to him lightly.

Since, Bonnie hadn't spent much time with her girls, she promised them they would all spend the weekend in DC. Tess's friend lived there and he said it was okay for them to stay at his house. Bonnie lied to Karl and told him that they'd be staying with Tess's aunt. She knew he wouldn't be cool with her staying at some guy's house. Bonnie didn't want to drive her old Sebring, so Karl rented her a red, mustang for the weekend, and gave her plenty of spending money. They left on a Friday afternoon and arrived in DC, around eight o' clock.

Even though they were all tired from the drive, they didn't let that get in their way. They changed clothes, and went straight to Dream Night Club. Dream was off the hook. There were five levels, and several VIP rooms. Bonnie, Tess, and Monique got into the club for free and invited into VIP. There was a private party being held there for one of the players from the Redskins. While, Tess and Monique were posted up with two major players, Bonnie was sneaking off to call Karl. She called him twice and didn't get an answer. After waiting a half hour for a call back, she snapped out of it and realized she should be enjoying herself. After three drinks, she let go completely. They danced all night long and nonstop. By the time they left Dream, their hair was all sweated out from dancing so hard. The club didn't close till four a.m., and right after, they went to a 24 hour diner with a few guys they met in VIP. Tess and Monique were really feeling their new DC friends. Though Bonnie tried not to show it, her mind was back on Karl again. She couldn't wait to get back home to him.

The next day, the girls were beat. They slept in all day and had intentions on going out to another club, until Bonnie received a call from Karl.

"Hey baby," Bonnie said.

"Baby, I'm in the hospital. I just crashed my fucking car," he said.

"What happened? Are you okay?"

"I fell asleep behind the wheel. Crashed my shit all up, fucked my neck up. The cops called the ambulance and damn near made me come here."

"I'm leaving now. I'm on my way baby," Bonnie said.

"You don't have to come back. I'm cool B," he said, trying to play it cool, knowing that he wanted her to get back.

"Yes, I do. I'm on my way," she said.

"Alright baby. I love you."

"Love you too."

Bonnie got back to Philly in no time. She dropped Tess and Monique off and went to Presbyterian Hospital. She wasn't expecting to see Karl lying on a small bed, in the hallway of the ER. She laughed to herself, when she saw how silly he looked wearing a neck brace and a ton of jewelry. His eyes were closed. Bonnie placed her hands on his chest. He opened his eyes, and just smiled when he saw her face.

"Baby, you can't be falling asleep behind the wheel. You could've killed yourself."

"I be running too much. I need to chill. And this Sarcoidosis be having me tired as hell," he said.

"Sarcoidosis?" Bonnie, asked with a concerned look on her face.

"It's a lung disease. I've had it all my life."

"My poor baby. You just need me to take care of you," she said, smiling.

"That's exactly what I need," he said.

"Where's your car?" Bonnie asked.

"My man Ted, had it towed to one of his body shops. He's into the car shit real heavy. He buys crashed cars, fixes em' up and then sells them," he said.

"Oh okay. That's what's up but that doesn't mean you can just go around, getting into accidents and stuff." They both laughed. "Seriously you gotta be more careful baby," she said.

Bonnie drove Karl home. She wasn't away two full days and his apartment was already a mess. She positioned Karl comfortably on the sofa and did some quick cleaning. She went upstairs to his bedroom to get ready for bed. She put on a tank top and a pair of his polo boxers. Just as she was leaving out of the bedroom, she couldn't help but notice the full trash can near the door. The first thing that stood out was a used condom. She bent down and took a closer look, to be sure her mind wasn't playing tricks on her. She picked up the condom and held it with her thumb and index finger. It was full of cum. Her heart sank down to her feet. She couldn't believe what she'd found. She ran down stairs, yelling and still holding the condom.

"What the fuck is this shit! You been fucking some other bitch? Oh, is that why you weren't picking up your phone last night, cause you was getting some pussy?" she screamed.

"Yo. You need to calm down. That's not mine. My boy was here last night, with some chick. I guess…"

Bonnie immediately cut him off. "Nigga stop lying. You want me to believe that you let him fuck a bitch in your bed?"

"What's wrong with that?" he said, trying to keep a straight face, while lying through his teeth.

"You know what, it's cool. Now that I know what type of shit you on, I'm gonna do me too. Don't get mad when I fuck somebody else!"

"Yo, you better watch your fucking mouth!" he said, while putting his finger in Bonnie's face.

"What you gonna do? Like I said, don't get mad when I fuck somebody else! I'm gonna give somebody all this young, tight pussy, since you wannna play games," she said.

The thought of Bonnie having sex with another man, made him furious. He blanked out, raised his hand and backhand slapped her. He slapped her so hard, that she fell to the floor.

"I told you not to fucking play with me! You think you can just say that you gon' fuck somebody else, and that it's cool?" he said, raising his voice.

Bonnie had never been hit by any man, not even her father. She lied there on the floor in complete shock. She realized she said some awful things, but she didn't deserve to be hit. She picked herself up from the floor, still crying. He tried to grab her and she pulled away from him and rushed upstairs to gather her things. Karl was still sore from the car accident, so he was a bit sluggish when going after her.

Bonnie went into the bedroom and started pulling her clothes out of the top two drawers.

"Bonnie, I'm sorry. Thinking about you being with somebody else makes me crazy," he said. "I'll never put my hands on you again."

"Karl I can't do this. This is too much too soon. I'm not doing this with you," she said, while looking into his eyes.

"Bonnie, listen. The condom was mine. I did have somebody here last night. I don't know why, I just did. And I'm sorry. I need you in my life." He sat on the edge of the bed and put both hands on top of his head. "Baby just give me a chance to show you I'm for real. Move in with me."

Bonnie didn't understand how this man was able to get inside her heart so fast. Even after everything that just transpired, she wasn't ready to leave him. She sat down on the bed next to him, not knowing what to say.

"B, I'm serious. I'll drive you home in the morning, to get all your stuff. I need you here with me," he said, while looking into her eyes.

"Okay. I'll move in," she said.

"I love you so much and I'm gonna prove it to you. You won't ever have to worry about anything like this again. I promise...I got you," he said. They kissed very passionately, and then wild, crazy sex followed. He held her in his arms all night long.

The next morning, Karl drove Bonnie home to get the rest of her things. When she walked in, her father was sitting on the couch watching television. She took a deep breath to prepare herself for the drama that was soon to come. She knew her father would be livid about her moving in with Karl. Since she'd been dating him her relationship with her father was not in a good place. He truly believed that Karl would only ruin his daughter's life.

"Daddy, I know you're not going to like what I'm about to tell you, but my mind is already made up. So, I just hope that you respect my decision."

"What is it now Bonnie?" he asked, with a concerned

expression on his face.

"I'm moving in with Karl."

"Sweetheart. Are you trying to throw your life away? I won't be able to sleep at night knowing that you're living with that man. I know the kind of life that he lives. Do you know what comes along with his lifestyle? You have no idea what you're getting yourself into," he said.

"Daddy, I'll be fine. I've spent enough time with him to know. I'm not going to throw my life away. I'm starting school next month. I'm still going to stick to my plans. Can you please just have some faith in me?"

"Bonnie if you leave with him, you're showing me that you have no respect for your father and if you walk out that door, don't bother coming back!" he said, adamantly.

"Fine. If that's the way you want it…then so be it," she said.

Bonnie dragged four large trash bags, stuffed with clothes, out on the front porch. Her father watched from the window, as Karl put the bags in the trunk of the car. Bonnie looked back at the house, before getting in the car. She saw her father leaving the window. Karl asked her if she was okay before pulling off. "Yes. I'm good baby," she said. As much as Bonnie loved her father, she wasn't going to let him or anyone else stand in the way of being with Karl. She was in love…crazy in love.

CHAPTER THREE
Upgrade You

Karl convinced Bonnie to quit her job at the Net. He made it very clear that he wanted to take care of her. She was hesitant at first, because she was just learning how to be independent. Bonnie actually enjoyed going to work every day and making her own money. He told her that if she worked fulltime, she wouldn't be able to concentrate on school. The underlying reason for Karl wanting her to quit was, he didn't want her around men all day. It wasn't that he was insecure. He just didn't like his chick being easy access.

Now that they were living together, Bonnie was sure Karl was all in. She didn't think he would move her in with him, if he wasn't ready to be in a committed relationship. It had only been a week since their altercation but she believed him when he told her it would never happen again. Bonnie didn't tell anyone what happened that night. Not even her two best friends. How could she tell them he hit her? Or that he was cheating on her. She didn't want anyone to look at him that way. Especially, since she knew she wasn't ready for it to be over between them.

Karl received a call from his friend Ted, letting him now he and Bonnie's cars were ready. They drove to Castle's Auto

Body on 23rd and Snyder in South Philly, to meet up with Ted. She had no idea Karl bought her a brand new car. She thought they were only going to pick up his Mercedes. Ted pulled up right behind them in a silver Cadillac DTS. He was short, light skinned, and had light green eyes. He would put you in mind of a heavier T.I.. He was handsome and could dress his ass off.

He jumped out of the car yelling out to Karl, "What's up playa!"

"What's up T!" Karl screamed back.

"You know me, just grinding. That's all," he said.

"Come meet my girl," Karl said, proudly.

Ted walked over to the passenger side to greet Bonnie. "How you doing?"

"Fine and you," she said, while shaking his hand.

"I'm good. I don't know what you did to my man over here, but you got his number! All he talk about is you," Ted said. Bonnie began blushing.

"Make sure you treat my man good alright!" he said.

"Oh for sure," she replied.

Karl and Ted stepped away from the car to have a sideline conversation.

"Karl, she bad as shit," Ted said.

"I know right. That's my baby right there," Karl said, with pride.

"Make sure you treat her right," he said.

"No doubt," he said and then they shook hands.

Karl was pleasantly surprised at the job Ted's people did on his car. There wasn't a single scratch on it. Karl and Ted went inside the auto shop to get tags and registration for Bonnie's 2002 Chevy Impala. Ted sold it to Karl for 10,000 dollars and he paid cash for it. He wanted to upgrade his baby into something nice and at the time Impalas were hot. Karl gave Bonnie the keys to her new car and told her he would meet her at the house later.

Bonnie couldn't believe Karl dropped ten stacks on a new car for her. She felt important to him and she couldn't of been happier. The first thing she did was pick up Monique and Tess, so they could cruise around the streets of Philly in her new ride. They drove around for hours, listening to music, laughing and talking like they always did. Monique told Bonnie to drive down North Philly, so she could check on her new guy friend, Shawn. Since she'd given him some, she claimed he was acting brand new. He went from calling her every day, to barely answering her calls. Monique said that she was going to play the hell out of him and she didn't care who was around. Bonnie and Tess just laughed. They were always down for a little fun.

When they pulled up on the block of 27th and Lehigh, Shawn was standing on the corner with a bunch of his homeboys. Bonnie pointed in his direction, "Ain't that him right there?"

"Yeah that's his black ass. Pull over," Monique said.

Monique jumped out of the car, fired up and ready for whatever. "Oh, so is this what you do?" You like to fuck bitches and then switch up on em!"

"Yo, you drawn! What you talkin' bout?" he asked.

"Nigga don't play. You know what I'm talkin' about. You been on my top all summer and now that I gave you some, your ass been MIA," she snapped back.

Bonnie and Tess sat in the car, amused by the whole scene. They loved seeing their girl wild out like this. They thought it was hilarious.

"You crazy as shit. It ain't like I been out here fucking with these bitches. I just been on some money shit," he explained.

"Well you better act like you know then!" she said, while turning her back towards him to walk away. He pulled her back and tried buttering her up some more. It wasn't like Monique was in her feelings over this guy. It was all fun and games to her. She turned away, switching her hips extra hard, while his eyes were fixed on her ass. She got back in the car and Bonnie peeled off so fast, that her tires screeched when she turned the corner. The three of them burst out into laughter and gave each other a high-five. "Bitch you crazy!" Bonnie yelled out, while laughing.

Bonnie anticipated a romantic evening with Karl that night. She was hoping they could take a nice, bubble bath together, followed by wild, passionate sex. He told her he would be home by nine. She put on a sexy two-piece lingerie set from Victoria's Secret and prepared a hot bath. She lit her favorite Jasmine Vanilla scented candles and placed them around the tub. She just knew it was going down, the second he walked in the door. She laid across the bed in her sexy lingerie and anxiously waited for Karl's arrival. It was eleven o' clock when she realized she fell asleep, and Karl still hadn't come home. She called his phone and didn't get an answer. An hour passed, she called again…still no answer. *Here we go again with this shit*, she thought to herself. She went into the bathroom, blew out the candles and drained the bathwater. She tried not to think the worst, but couldn't stop the negative thoughts that crept into her head. *What could he be doing this late and why wouldn't he be answering my calls? Is he with another woman?* Bonnie got back into bed and tried to calm herself down. She stared at the clock every five minutes, waiting for him to walk through the door.

In the early morning, Karl crept into their bedroom. He'd taken his clothes off in the hallway, so that he wouldn't wake Bonnie. He slowly climbed into bed and wrapped his arms around her. Bonnie opened her eyes, looked at the clock and saw that it was 4:30.

"Where have you been?"

"I was taking care of business baby."

"This late Karl?" she asked, while turning towards him.

"Baby don't start. I was out making moves. I wasn't with anybody if that's what you're thinking," he said.

"I didn't say that." She said. "I was worried about you."

"Don't worry about me baby. I know what I'm doing out here. I'm gon' always make it home to you. I promise," Karl said. He kissed her on the forehead and told her that he loved her.

"I love you too," she said, and that was it. She didn't dig any further. Even though she believed he was doing more than just handling business, she didn't want to nag him about it. She let it ride but just this one time.

Over the next few weeks, Bonnie prepared for school. She got a notice in the mail stating that she received the maximum of financial aid and that it still left a balance on her account. She was told by a financial aid advisor that if the balance of four thousand wasn't paid, before the end of the first week of class; then there would be a hold placed on her account. She was really stressing, because a hold on her account would prevent her from attending classes.

Bonnie didn't want to ask Karl for the money. She didn't want him to think she was the kind of chick that always had her hand out. It wasn't about what she could gain from him. She wasn't with him for the money. Bonnie genuinely loved him and she wanted him to know that.

As much as she didn't want to bother Karl with her financial problems, she didn't have anyone else to turn to for that kind of money. When she told Karl she needed his help, he didn't hesitate at all. They walked into Drexel University, and stood in the bursar's office line for over an hour together. Karl paid the balance in full, and in cash.

Bonnie's Birthday was coming up in three days and the start of school was less than two weeks away, so Karl wanted to do something special for her. He decided to take her on a vacation. And though, Bonnie looked good whenever she stepped out, Karl wanted to upgrade her wardrobe to his taste level. He took her to Neiman Marcus, and the Gucci store at King of Prussia Mall. These were two of his favorite places to shop. He told Bonnie to do her thing and get whatever she wanted. He bought her a few pairs of Manolo Blahniks, jeans by True Religion, Frankie B, Rock & Republic, and BCBG. She fell in love with a gold, metallic Gucci Hobo bag. She looked at Karl and said, "Baby it cost two thousand dollars." She was under the impression that it was too expensive. "It's cool. Get it," he said. "Oh and before we leave, we gotta get some swimwear."

"For what?" she asked.

"Because we're going to Hawaii tomorrow," he replied.

"What! Are you serious? Hawaii!" she said, ecstatically. "I've never been to Hawaii before."

"Me neither," he said. "Everything already paid for. Flight and hotel. We outta here in the morning."

"Oh my God! I can't wait!" she said. Bonnie stood on the tip of her toes and wrapped her arms around his neck. "Karl, I love you so much."

"I love you too B," he said.

Bonnie was lost in amazement. Every day with Karl was like a new adventure and she loved it. He went out of his way to let her know she was important to him. Bonnie felt as though she had truly found her prince charming, and all she hoped for was a happy ending.

The next day, after a twelve and a half hour flight, Karl and Bonnie arrived at Kahului Airport, on the island of Maui. They took a shuttle to the Grand Wailea resort, where they'd be staying for the next four days.

The resort was magnificent and their villa looked even better than the brochures. It was like paradise. It included three bedrooms, three bath, a large kitchen, with new amenities, a private sandy beach entrance and an outdoor barbecue area. The resort featured six restaurants, a luxurious spa, several pools, and upscale shopping.

Bonnie and Karl were both exhausted from their long flight, and all they wanted was relaxation. Bonnie changed into a floral maxi dress. Karl was topless and wearing a pair of yellow linen shorts. They laid in a hammock, with their arms wrapped around one another.

"Isn't this nice?" Bonnie asked.

"Yeah it is. It feels so good to be out here with you," he replied.

"Thank you so much for bringing me here. And thank you for helping me with school. You have no idea what that means to me," she said.

"You're welcome baby. I'd do anything for you," he said. "You know what's crazy?"

"What?"

"I prayed for someone like you. And God answered my prayers. I'm so happy that I found you…it's like you were made for me."

"I feel the same way about you. I never felt this way about anyone before," she said.

"I'm not even gon' lie to you. I've been with a lot of women but I've never been with anyone like you. You're my fucking baby," he said. "Now that I got you, you good. I promise you that. Just promise me one thing."

"What's that?" she asked.

"That you'll never leave me…no matter what comes our way. Promise me you gon' be right here by my side," he said, in a serious tone.

"Karl, I'll never leave you. Not ever. This is how it's gon' always be. Just you and me." He kissed her on the forehead, like he always did and she laid her head on his chest. They stayed out there all night, watching the ocean, talking, while enjoying the beautiful Hawaiian breeze.

The next day, Karl didn't want to waste anytime jumping into some action. He wanted to go snorkeling and scuba diving. Bonnie wasn't a good swimmer and didn't like the idea of being under water. She tried her best to talk him out of it.

"I know you not a lil' punk," he said jokingly.

"I'll go snorkeling but I'm not scuba diving in that water. They have sharks out here boy," she said, with both hands on her hips.

A kayaking tour was part of the snorkeling package, so they took advantage of that. They toured across Olowalu, which is a beach stretch, located on the west side of the island of Maui. Their tour guide was a native Hawaiian and he took pride in finding them sea turtles, octopus, and tropical fish, while snorkeling. Karl was just as excited as Bonnie to be swimming along all the sea creatures. It was an experience both Karl and Bonnie would never forget.

Later that day, they went back to their hotel to get changed. Bonnie put on a sheer cheetah print dress from BCBG and she paired it with her new black Chanel slides. She wore her hair down, with a part in the middle. Karl wore an aloha style shirt, a pair of khaki shorts and Louis Vuitton flip flops. They went to Humuhumu, which is one of the finest restaurants, located inside The Grand hotel. They were seated outside on the deck, where there was a live performance. There was traditional music playing and beautiful girls hula dancing. Since they were undecided on the menu, Karl told the waiter to bring out their most popular dishes. They were served Malaysian Style Marinated Lamb, Tasmanian Salmon, Seared Ahi, Blue Crab, Grilled Vegetables and Tofu Skewers. For dessert, they had chocolate cake with Kalua coffee ice cream.

Bonnie sat at the dinner table in awe with her man. Just being in a beautiful place like Hawaii with Karl felt surreal. She couldn't believe she almost passed up on him. If it weren't for Tess and Monique, then she would've never gotten with Karl.

Karl and Bonnie got wasted off of Humuhumu's famous Tsunami drink. They were both feeling in the mood and couldn't wait to get back to their villa to get busy. Karl practically ripped Bonnie's clothes off that night. They brought in Bonnie's birthday on the beach, making love. It had to be something in the air that night because Bonnie was a beast. She completely took control and went crazy on Karl. She licked all over his abdomen while admiring his physique. It was such a turn on to her, how in shape he was. She licked all over his body, paying special attention to his penis. They went from making sweet love, to having wild and rough sex…all night long.

It was a much needed vacation for the both of them, especially Karl. It allowed him to escape the harsh realities of being a street hustler. He dealt with so much on the streets and most of the time, it had him stressed out to the highest degree. Sometimes he felt like the world was against him, and that he couldn't trust anyone. There was a part of his life and a side to him, that Bonnie hadn't seen yet. It was a side that he wasn't proud of, and one that she would soon be introduced to.

CHAPTER FOUR
Slippin'

Back In Philly…

"**Y**o," Karl said, answering his cell phone.

"Aye yo. That white bitch wasn't cool. Every time I drop her, she loose," said the voice on the other end of the phone, speaking in code.

"St. Claire get the fuck outta here with that shit. You're the only nigga complaining. All my homeys say she fucking like a mutha fucka," Karl said.

"Well she ain't get wet for me. I'm running that bitch back!" St. Claire said.

"Dog! I'm not taking her back. Matter of fact, get off my phone with this shit. Meet me at Fairmount Park in an hour!" Karl said, raising his voice.

"Yeah. Whatever nigga," he said.

Karl sold St. Claire a brick of cocaine for 21,500, the day before. He believed Karl sold him coke that was compressed. After cooking it, it wouldn't get hard and if you had good coke on your hands, it would easily rock up. Some dealers were into cutting coke with baking soda, and then re-bricking to make it appear less cut. Karl wasn't into that though and he took it very personal that St. Claire was even accusing him of doing some sucker shit like that.

"Fuck was that nigga talkin' bout?" Mehki asked.

Mehki was Karl's right hand man. He was a wild dude, who was described by most as a young gun. Reckless, evil and always looking for a reason.

"He saying that the coke I gave him wasn't cool. First time I heard that shit," Karl said.

"That nigga always on some nut shit. You should let me see that nigga," Mehki said.

"We gon' shoot down there to meet him in an hour. We'll see what he's talkin' bout then," Karl replied.

Karl and Mehki stopped at Yummy Diner on 52nd and Arch St, for breakfast. Karl was still upset about St. Claire's accusations and he couldn't wait to see him face to face. They weren't the best of friends, but they had known each other for quite some time and did a lot of business together. Karl didn't want to see the situation get out of hand. He was hoping they could settle things, especially since Mehki wanted to off him so badly already.

After leaving the diner, Karl and Mehki went to Fairmount Park to meet with St. Claire. They parked on Parkside Ave, where they usually met and waited for him to show up. It wasn't like St. Claire to not be on time, so after twenty minutes of waiting and unanswered calls, Karl knew that he wasn't coming.

Karl did find it strange that St. Claire didn't call to say that he couldn't make it, but he didn't read too much into it. He figured that he probably got caught up doing something else and lost track of time. Mehki felt like something was shady about this guy but he kept it to himself. He was always suspicious of everyone, but this time his senses were on point.

Later that night, when Karl was on his way home, he stopped down 39th and Aspen to pick up a few thousand one of his workers owed him. After collecting his money, he turned down a small block, so he could make his way through the zoo and onto Highway 76.

As soon as he got to the end of the block, he spotted a black Caprice with tinted windows on the corner, with the lights turned off. Before Karl could make his left turn to go over the 39th St. bridge gun shots were fired at his vehicle. Pop! Pop! Pop! Pop! Karl ducked his head, while still turning the steering wheel. He pressed the gas pedal to the floor and tried to make it off the tight block without getting hit. Pop! Pop! Two more shots were fired and this time a bullet tore through the rear window, shattering glass everywhere.

As soon as Karl got to the Bridge, he heard police sirens. In spite of the countless shots fired at his vehicle, he was able to make it onto the expressway untouched. *I'ma kill this nigga* Karl thought to himself, referring to St. Claire. He had a flashback to 1996, him lying on the sidewalk, in a puddle of his own blood, after being shot six times, by a cat named Jabril. A petty argument between two hot heads that had gone bad. "You should've killed me muthafucka," Karl said, right before shooting Jabril six times, leaving him lifeless. It wasn't the first life that he'd taken and it damn sure wouldn't be the last.

Before Karl parked his car, he circled the block a few times to be sure everything was cool. When he got inside, Bonnie was lying on the sofa waiting for him. He wasn't sure if he should tell her what just happened. He didn't want to scare her but he didn't want to keep her in the dark either.

"B, I gotta talk to you."

"What's up baby?"

"Somebody was just shooting at me."

"What! Who was shooting at you?" she asked.

"I know exactly who it was. I'ma handle it though. He made a big mistake, not killing me," he said.

"What do you mean you're gonna handle it? I don't want you getting hurt. I'll lose my mind if something happened to you," she said.

"B, I know what I'm doing, just trust me. Everything is gon' be just fine," he said, while wrapping his arms around her.

"You're so much better than this. These streets don't deserve you. You shouldn't have to live like this," she said, in a sad tone."

"To live is to suffer and to survive, well that's to find meaning in the suffering," he said, quoting one of his favorite rappers, DMX.

Karl definitely suffered a lot in the cold world that he was living. He still hadn't quite found the meaning in the suffering, however. Less than 24 hours later, Karl retaliated against St. Claire, leaving him lifeless. He received a call from a friend telling him that St. Claire was playing ball at a playground in West Philly. He sent Mehki to take care of him and he was more than happy to oblige.

CHAPTER FIVE
Stranger In My House

A few months passed and Bonnie was just getting settled into college life. She successfully completed her first semester with a 4.0 gpa. Bonnie following through with her college plans is what made her father come around. Michael still wasn't pleased about she and Karl's relationship but Bonnie was just happy that he was finally speaking to her again. He thought Bonnie would get comfortable with Karl and so wrapped up in his world that she would lose herself, but so far Bonnie was on the right track.

Karl started getting his kids every other weekend and since he was gone a lot, they spent most of their time with Bonnie. She took them skating, to the movies, and amusement parks, or sometimes she would stay in with them and have game night. She always found something entertaining to do with them. She enjoyed having them around, and she formed a close bond with both of them.

One morning, Karl left the house to walk his two pit bulls. Bonnie noticed he left his cell phone on the dresser. She was hesitant to look in it at first, because she had a gut feeling she would find something that would hurt her. All she could hear was a voice in her head, saying *Bonnie don't go looking for something, because you just might find it.* Curiosity was eating away at her and she didn't know when she'd have that chance again, since he kept his phone glued to him at all times.

The minute she picked up his cell phone her heart starting racing. There was a picture mail notification flashing on the home screen, from someone named Sasha. She opened the message and couldn't believe what appeared before her eyes. It was a picture of her standing in front of a mirror naked, followed by a text message, *Don't you miss all of this.*

She went into his other downloads and media folder. There were so many pictures of naked women but what really pushed Bonnie over the edge was the video she found. Karl recorded two girls performing oral sex on him. At first, she was unsure if it was him in the video but in the end, after he ejaculated in their mouths, she heard his voice and caught a glimpse of his huge K necklace, hanging from his neck.

Bonnie wasn't brave enough to look any further. She seen enough and became overwhelmed by a rush of intense emotions. She paced back and forth in their bedroom, anxiously waiting for Karl to walk through the door.

Hurt and confused, Bonnie sat down on the edge of the bed. She heard laughter coming from the living room and was quickly reminded Karl's children were still there. Knowing it wasn't the time to get into a fight with Karl, she tried to calm herself down but everything changed when Karl stepped into their bedroom.

"You're a fucking liar. And I'm the biggest dummy to believe all this shit you tell me, about how much you love me," she said, while pulling her clothes out of the drawer.

"What now Bonnie!" he said. "What the fuck are you talkin' about now!"

"I'm talkin' about the naked bitches in your phone, I'm talkin' about the two nasty stripper looking bitches, you had sucking on your dick!" she screamed. "That's what I'm talkin' about!"

"You went in my phone?" he asked. "That wasn't me. My homey sent that to me, because one of the chicks is from around the way and she always acting like she hot shit. We just laughing at that bitch…that's all."

"First of all, I saw your damn necklace, and I know your voice Karl. Second of all who the fuck is Sasha? Matter of fact, I don't even care, I'm over this shit!" she said, still pulling her clothes from the drawers.

Karl lunged at Bonnie, wrapped his left hand around her neck and then punched her in the face. She managed to recover from the blow rather quickly. She picked herself up from the floor and charged back at him. She swung at him with all her might but missed him. He then pushed her down on the floor and forced himself on top of her, to restrain her from throwing another punch.

"Calm the fuck down, don't you know I will fucking kill you in here Bonnie!" he yelled.

"With your kids in the other room? Get off of me. I fucking hate you!" she, said while tears rolled down her face.

"I hate you too! And I don't care who's in the other room. Don't fucking play with me. It's not like you caught me with a bitch. You went snooping through my shit," he said.

"You can do whatever you want. Just let me go. I'm ready to gracefully bow out of this relationship Karl."

"As much as I go through out in the streets, I don't need to come home and fight with you over dumb shit. I don't care about these bitches," he said. "You want to know the truth? Fine! I met those bitches at a strip club. I gave em' a hundred dollars apiece. That's it! All they did was suck my dick. I don't give a damn about those bitches!"

Karl started picking Bonnie's clothes up from the floor, attempting to place them back in the dresser drawers. Bonnie still angry, snatched the clothes out of his hand.

"So is that supposed to make me feel better? Because it doesn't. I'm disgusted with you Karl," she said, while shaking her head.

"I don't know why I'm fucking up like this. I don't deserve you. You're the best thing that ever happened to me and I'm putting my hands on you. I ain't shit Bonnie! You deserve better than me," he said.

Karl sat down on the floor, with his back leaning against the dresser and knees pulled up to his chest. He felt so disappointed in himself and he thought it would be over this time for sure. Once again he lost his self-control and hit Bonnie after promising her he would never do it again.

Sadly enough, Bonnie began to feel sorry for Karl. Although she was the one lied to, cheated on, and given a black eye, deep down inside she was sad for him. Hearing those words come out of his mouth *I ain't shit Bonnie*, really struck a chord with her. She knew Karl had inner demons, but she was willing to help him fight them. She believed that if she stayed by his side, and loved him hard enough, everything would get better.

Bonnie hugged Karl, and told him they would get through it together. They sat on the floor, in the same position for almost an hour, just holding each other. Karl told Bonnie he loved her and he would make everything right again. "Just don't give up on us," he said.

Karl went in the front room to check on the kids and from the looks of things they hadn't heard a thing. They were laughing and playing video games. Karl told the kids to get their bags ready, so that he could drive them home. He prevented the kids from seeing Bonnie and her black eye, by telling them she wasn't feeling well.

While Karl was out, Bonnie called her mother Karen for advice. She knew that her mother would be able to relate to what she was going through and she was in desperate need of some guidance. After Bonnie told her mother what happened, she told Bonnie it wasn't a good idea to stay with him. Karen believed that his behavior would only get worse and she feared for her daughter's safety. She even warned Bonnie he would say and do anything in order for her to forgive him.

"Mom it's really not like that at all. He's a good person but everyone makes mistakes. What happened doesn't define who he is," she said.

"You're right baby everybody makes mistakes, but remember it's only a mistake if it happens once," Karen replied.

"I know mom and I'll keep that in mind but I love him and as of right now I'm going to ride it out with him."

"Well baby, I can't talk you out of loving him. I just want you to be smart and just know that I love you. You be sure to let me know if anything like this happens again and remember you can always come here with me if you need to get away," she said.

"Yes I know. Thank you for listening. I love you mom. Oh, and one more thing before I go…please keep this between us."

"It's always between us baby, and I love you too," she replied.

What Bonnie loved the most about her mother, was that she could talk to her about anything. Their relationship was beyond a mother and daughter relationship. She could open up with her mother as if she was one of her girlfriends. She never held anything back and she didn't have to worry about being judged or looked at differently.

A few weeks passed, and she and Karl still weren't on the right track. He was spending more time away from home, which led Bonnie to believe that he was out with other women. Even when he was home, Bonnie felt as though he was very distant. After having a talk with Monique and Tess, she realized she needed to get more into herself and stop worrying so much about what Karl was doing.

Bonnie started hanging out with her girls more often and she even got back in touch with her friend Jay. She completely cut him off when she and Karl got serious, but now she was starting to really miss his friendship. She and Jay never slept together, because he had a girlfriend when they met. Even though he still wanted to get with Bonnie, she wasn't into sleeping with somebody else's man. So, they kept things strictly platonic. They were like best friends, before Karl came along and shut everything down.

Usually when Bonnie was home alone and bored, she would call Karl a bunch of times and press him about what time he was coming home. Not this Saturday night. She got dressed and met Monique and Tess at a neighborhood bar, in West Philly. They ordered some food and had a couple of drinks and from there, they headed to Palmer Night Club.

At Palmer's they had a ball. It had been a while since the three of them went clubbing together and they were wilding out. They drank and danced all night long. Not one time did Karl's whereabouts cross Bonnie's mind. She was too busy enjoying herself.

When Bonnie got home, Karl was already there and him beating her home was definitely a first. It made Bonnie feel good seeing his car parked in front of the door. She wanted him to know she wasn't going to just sit in the house, while he ran the streets and did whatever he wanted.

Bonnie staggered up onto the front porch and before she could even turn the key, Karl opened the door and stared her down with angry eyes. The look in his eyes was all too familiar and she just knew it was about to go down, as soon as she got inside.

"Where the fuck you been?" he asked. "It's 3:00 in the morning!"

"I went out with Monique and Tess," she said, as she walked past him and through the door. "What's the problem?"

"You think it's cool for you to just walk your ass in here this late?" he said, raising his voice.

"You do it to me all the time," she replied.

"I'm a man. You can't do what the fuck I do. Your place is at home, not in the fucking streets and you walking in here all drunk and shit!" he screamed.

"Karl I'm not going to argue with you. It won't happen again, alright?"

"Give me your phone," he said.

"For what?" she asked.

"What you mean for what! Give me the fucking phone!"

Although Bonnie wasn't cheating on Karl, the last thing she wanted was for him to see text messages from Jay. There weren't any inappropriate messages, but she knew Karl would lose it if he found out she was still in contact with him.

She took a deep breath and handed him her cell phone. He snatched the phone from her and started looking though her call history. He then scrolled through her text messages. Bonnie tried to talk him out of looking any further.

"I can't believe you don't trust me," she said. "Can I have my phone back?"

Karl just ignored her until he came across Jay's text messages. The name stuck out like a sore thumb as he was scrolling through her messages. He knew Jay from around the way and they were cool, before he found out that he was friends with Bonnie. Now he couldn't stand him and seeing their text messages back and forth, made Karl furious.

"You still talking to that nut ass nigga Jay?"

"Huh?" she said, trying to collect her thoughts.

"You heard what the fuck I said!"

"Not really. I just texted him to see how he was doing…that's all."

Karl called Jay's phone, and told Bonnie that he was about to check him for even disrespecting him.

"Hello," Jay said, half sleep.

"Yo, nigga this Karl."

"What's up," he said.

"Don't be calling or texting my bitch phone. I don't play no games with her!"

"It ain't even like that, we just…" Before Jay could even finish his sentence Karl interrupted him.

"Fuck all that. You heard what the fuck I said!" Karl hung up the phone before Jay had a chance to get another word in.

"You gon' get your boy fucked up Bonnie," he said.

"Baby I promise you we're just friends," she replied.

"I heard what you said and I'm telling you it ain't no room for that nigga."

"Okay baby. I won't talk to him anymore. It's a wrap," she said.

She moved in close to him and wrapped her arms around his neck. She looked up at him and stared deeply into his eyes. As crazy as it sounds, seeing Karl get so jealous turned her on. She kissed him passionately on the lips and he quickly removed her clothes. One thing they loved the most about each other was their sexual chemistry. They would have crazy fights, and say the most awful things to one another, but then they would make love like it would be their last time.

A few days later, Monique called Bonnie and asked her to go shopping with her. Karl kept money stashed throughout the house and Bonnie had access to every single dollar. She took a couple thousand from one of his stashes and stuffed it into her Chanel pocketbook and headed out the door.

Bonnie was on her way to meet up with Monique in West Philly, when a woman pulled up on the side of her, in a red Honda Accord. From what Bonnie could see, the woman appeared to be very attractive. She blew the horn, rolled down her passenger window and motioned for Bonnie to do the same.

"Hey excuse me. Is this Karl's car?" the woman asked.

"Yeah, Why? What's up!" Bonnie asked, with a frown on her face.

"Just making sure," she said.

"Who are you? And how do you know him?"

Her car was easy to recognize because she had a Drexel University sticker in the rear window. She and Karl switched cars a lot, so Bonnie assumed that he'd been around this woman, while he was in her car.

The woman didn't answer Bonnie's questions. She rolled her window up and peeled off down Girard Avenue. Bonnie knew Karl had dealings with this woman and she was pissed off about it. She pulled over on 42nd and Girard, and Monique drove up shortly after.

"Girl you won't believe this shit!" Bonnie said to

Monique, as she was getting into the car.

"What girl?" Monique asked.

"Some bitch just stopped me and asked if this was Karl's car. So, I was like yeah, why and who are you…and she just drove off."

"Are you serious? You should've followed that hoe," Monique said.

"Yeah I know right. Monique, I'm not even gonna lie to you, I'm so sick of Karl and his shit. I love him but every time I turn around, I'm catching him in some shit," she said.

"Girl that's how these niggas are, especially the ones that are getting to a dollar. If this is the life you want, there are some things you have to deal with and these thirsty bitches are part of that equation," she said. "Karl loves you, he doesn't give a fuck about these bitches. You're who he comes home to every night. Don't let these hoes come between what ya'll got."

"I hear what you're saying Monique, but Karl is the only one that can let these chicks come between what we got. I'm gonna ride for him, but at the end of the day, I need to know that he's riding for me too," she said.

Bonnie decided she wasn't going to mention it to Karl. He would never own up to it and Bonnie felt as though it wasn't even worth discussing. Him denying he knew the woman, would only get Bonnie heated and then they would find themselves in another fight. So she did a little therapeutic shopping, and hung out with Monique all day.

Monique had a new man in her life Bonnie hadn't met yet. His name was Art, and he was a professional heavy weight boxer, from North Philly. For the first time, Monique found someone who was able to handle her wild ways and feistiness.

Monique told Bonnie about the countless girls who tried to get in the way of their relationship. She'd been receiving prank calls from blocked numbers, and was even told by one girl if she didn't leave Art alone, she was going to put her in the hospital. But Monique wasn't shook one bit. She told them she was the wrong chick to be messed with and if they tried her, she would put them in a body bag first. When Bonnie asked her how she was able to put up with so much drama, she replied "Shit I knew what I was getting myself into. It's all part of the game." Sadly enough, Bonnie would soon adapt this very same attitude when dealing with Karl.

It was Dec 31, 2002, and Bonnie just knew she would be bringing in the new year with her man. She spent the entire day prepping for the night, making sure her nails were done, hair tossed and she had an outfit that would shut any party down.

When Karl came home, he put two bottles of champagne in the freezer, then hurried back out and drove off with his friends. He didn't even say a word to her. It was already 10 o'clock, and he still hadn't said anything about where they'd be going, so she called him on his cell phone.

"What's up baby?" he said.

"Where you going?" she asked.

"I gotta make a couple runs, I'll be back."

"Well, should I start getting dressed? she asked. "We're bringing in New Years together right?"

"Baby, me and the boys riding over to A.C. tonight. I thought you probably wanted to hang out with your girlfriends."

"Karl just say that you want to hang out with your friends, because it has nothing to do with me wanting to hang out with mines," she said, in a very irritated voice. "I wanted to be with you tonight."

"Here we go again. You always complaining about something," he said.

"I'm complaining because I want to bring in the New Year with you Karl?"

"Yeah! You need to learn how to chill. If you learn to do that, we'll be good," he said.

"You're right and starting right now, I'm going to chill," she said sarcastically.

Bonnie hung up the phone and for a split second she

thought about going out with her girls but she knew she wouldn't enjoy herself. Bonnie wasn't feeling Karl's new attitude and it made her feel very insecure about herself. Why would he choose to spend New Year's Eve with his friends, instead of her? Did he make plans with another woman? And did he still love her the same? These were all the questions that left Bonnie feeling uneasy and uncertain. She stayed in all night and watched the ball drop in Times Square, from her king size bed.

Two weeks had gone by and Bonnie still hadn't forgot Karl spent New Year's Eve and New Year's day away from home. He had the audacity to walk in the door the next day, at 6 o'clock in the evening, like he did nothing wrong.

Bonnie was fed up with Karl and wanted to give him a taste of his own medicine. She got dressed, left the house and then waited an hour before she put her plan in motion. "Hey Tess. What you doing?"

"Nothing girl, just chilling."

"I need you to do me a favor. Block your number out, call Karl and tell him you seen his girl at Friday's with another guy," she said. Tess laughed. "Why you want me to do that girl?"

"Because I just want to fuck with his head a little bit. Since, he's always playing with mine. He been on some bullshit lately and I want to give him a reality check," Bonnie said.

Tess had to call Karl twice, before he picked up and he answered the phone in an angry manner, "Who the fuck is this calling me from a blocked number?"

"Your girl at Friday's right now with another dude. I was just calling to let you know," Tess said, disguising her voice.

"Who is this? he asked. "My girl ain't with no other nigga," he said, in disbelief.

"Yeah okay. I'm just calling to look out that's all."

"Which Friday's?" he asked.

"The one up City Line," she said.

Karl hung up and immediately called Bonnie's phone.

She purposely didn't answer. She wanted him to sweat a little bit and think maybe she was with someone else. He was getting too comfortable and Bonnie wanted to remind him that if he could play, she could to. She laughed with Tess, as he called her phone repeatedly. She waited til' after the fifth phone call before she answered.

"Hey baby," she said, in a calm voice.

"Where you at?" he asked, eagerly.

"I'm at Tess's house."

"How long you been there?"

"I been here for a while," she said. "Why what's wrong?"

"Nothing just come home. I miss you," he said.

"Okay, I'll be right there," she said.

Bonnie hung up the phone and she and Tess burst out into laughter. She could hear the worry in his voice and she loved it. He believed Bonnie when she told him she was with Tess, because he drove to Friday's to see if she was there. He was ready to go off and act a fool if he saw Bonnie with another man.

That night when Bonnie got home she and Karl had a long talk. He promised her he was going to get his act together and things would be back to how it was when they first met. He also told Bonnie that a lot of their problems stemmed from what he was dealing with on the streets. He wanted her to know it had nothing to do with other women.

This wasn't the first time they had one of these talks, so she didn't really believe too much of what he was saying. At this point, she was thinking *Actions speak much louder than words.* And boy did his actions contradict his words.

Bonnie was back in school for the Spring semester. She would normally have class all day and wouldn't be home till after 5pm. But one day, Bonnie came home earlier than usual. She opened the door and disabled the house alarm. Suddenly, she heard commotion coming from the living room and then a few male voices. She walked through their long hallway and into their living room and saw Karl, Mehki and two unfamiliar faces, sitting on the sofa, with bricks of cocaine and tons of money on the coffee table.

"What the fuck are you doing here?" Karl asked.

"What the fuck you mean, what am I doing here?" she spat back. "I live here!"

"Go in the fucking room Bonnie!" he yelled.

"Don't talk to me like that. I'm not your child!" she said, as she turned and walked away.

Karl immediately raised from the sofa and rushed towards Bonnie, gripping her up by her arm and pulling her into their bedroom.

"What did I tell you about talking to me crazy?"

"What? Karl, you're crazy," she said. "I come home and you cursing me out for no reason and in front of your friends. I'm so sick of this up and down shit with you."

"Watch your fucking mouth!" he yelled.

"Karl we need a break from each other. I'm not happy anymore and all we do is argue," she said, in a sad voice. "I think we just need some time apart.

"Fuck it then Bonnie, you can go. I won't stop you," he said, trying to put on a front. "But when you leave, you're not taking my car."

"Your car? You're so petty. Fuck you and that car," she spat.

Bonnie packed a couple of bags and called Monique to come get her. Monique said it was okay to stay at her house for as long as she needed. Bonnie was mentally drained from the emotional rollercoaster she'd been on lately. She needed to be away from him, so she could clear her head.

The first night away from Karl, she didn't answer any of his calls. She loved him deeply, but was seriously considering calling it quits. She thought about all of the things her dad was trying to warn her about. Her entire world revolved around Karl and when they weren't right...nothing was right. At this point, school wasn't even a priority.

After two nights of completely ignoring Karl, Bonnie grew weak and started to miss him tremendously. He left numerous voicemails, telling her how much he loved her and wanted her to come home. Bonnie packed her bags into Monique's car and drove home. Her plan was to go home, make up with Karl, then have him follow her back to Monique's to return her car.

It was about 11 o'clock in the morning, when Bonnie stepped foot in the door. She disabled the alarm, and before she could close the door behind her, Karl rushed out of their bedroom frantic and drenched in sweat. It didn't take Bonnie long to figure out there was someone else in the bedroom.

She barged her way into their bedroom and saw a young naked girl lying in their bed. The moment she entered the room she could smell sex in the air. Bonnie became furious. She leaped across the room, onto the bed and attacked the girl like she was going to kill her. Bonnie gave her several blows to the face before Karl pulled her off of the girl and even then, she was still swinging.

Karl pushed Bonnie out of the room and into the hallway. Bonnie walked into the living room and saw the girl's clothes all over the floor. Tears just streamed down Bonnie's face. She couldn't believe this was happening. She didn't recognize the man standing in front of her. How could he disrespect her in that way? Bonnie was truly hurt to her heart. She stormed out of the house and Karl followed behind her.

"Bonnie, I'm sorry," he said. "Just let me talk to you for a second."

"Karl, I don't know who you are anymore. How could you do this to me?" she said, hardly able to finish her sentences.

"I was missing you. I called you a bunch of times, and you weren't returning my calls. I didn't know what else to do."

"So you brought someone to our house and fucked her in our bed?" she said, while crying. "I don't want nothing to do with you. I'm done."

"Bonnie, I'm sorry. I really fucked up this time," he said.

"Yeah, you did, so why don't you go back in there with that bitch, because I don't want you anymore. I'm moving on for real this time," she said.

Bonnie left Karl standing at the bottom of the stairs. She got into the car and then sped off. The pain she felt was deep down in the pit of her stomach. *How could he do this to me?* Is what she kept asking herself, over and over again. She couldn't stop the tears from rolling down her face. She knew there was no way she could ever take him back. This time he'd gone too far and the damage done was way beyond repair.

CHAPTER SIX
Break up 2 Make Up

Two weeks later...

Bonnie was under so much stress she hadn't realized she missed her period, until she began feeling nauseous and fatigued. Bonnie, Tess, and Monique all sat together in the waiting room of Planned Parenthood, praying that she wasn't pregnant.

"Bonnie Summers," the nurse called out. Bonnie stood nervously, and followed the nurse to the back.

She took Bonnie into the counseling room to ask her several questions, regarding sexual history, date of her last menstrual, and whether or not she would keep the baby if she were pregnant. After she answered all of the nurse's questions, she instructed Bonnie to give a urine sample.

Having a baby was the last thing she wanted at this point in her life. She hadn't spoken to Karl in two weeks, and she didn't plan on talking to him anytime soon. He called her numerous times, sent text messages and left voicemails apologizing for what he'd done. It took everything inside of her not to answer any of his calls. She still loved him very much, and if it hadn't been for Monique and Tess keeping her occupied, then she would've already gone back to him.

The nurse returned back to the room. When she closed the door behind her and sat back down, Bonnie knew what she was going to say, before the words came out of her mouth.

"Okay, Bonnie," she said. "The pregnancy test was positive."

"Are you serious?" she said. "I can't believe this."

"Yes and based on your last menstrual, you're about five weeks."

"Do you know if you're going to keep it?" she asked.

"I'm not one hundred percent sure, but more than likely I'm going to," she replied.

"If you change your mind, give us a call and we can discuss abortion and all of your options with you," she said. "But in the meantime, I'm going to prescribe you some prenatal vitamins."

"Okay. Thank you."

Bonnie, Tess, and Monique walked out of the doctor's office in complete shock.

"What are you going to do?" Tess asked.

"I don't know. This was certainly not part of the plan, but I don't want to get an abortion," she said.

"I think you should keep it." Tess replied.

"Yeah, me too," Monique added.

"I want to. I'm just scared. Karl and I are over and now I'm carrying his baby. I'm in my first year of college, and my grades are already slipping," she said. "Everything is a mess right now."

"Bonnie, everything will work itself out and I think this baby will only bring you two closer. I think you should call him right now," Tess said.

"I don't know," she replied. "Maybe you guys are right."

Bonnie was determined to ignore Karl for as long as she could, but since finding out that she was pregnant, she became vulnerable once again. She called Karl the next morning and he answered on the first ring. He was so happy to hear from her. She told him she was pregnant and confused as to what to do about it. Karl told her he wanted the baby more than anything in the world and that it was exactly what he needed to keep himself focused and out of trouble. Bonnie just held the phone and let him do all the talking. He told her he loved her and he wanted her to come home. He promised Bonnie he would do whatever it took to make things right between them.

And just like that Karl was back in again. He picked Bonnie up from Monique's house and brought her home. It was weird for Bonnie walking into the house that day. She could still see herself barging into the room, and catching a naked girl in their bed. Bonnie walked into their bedroom and saw Karl bought her a bouquet of flowers and a card. On the front of the card there was a figure of a pregnant woman, with the words congratulations in cursive, and in the inside Karl wrote, "I love you more than you know. You're my world! My everything!

Karl hugged Bonnie tight and kissed her on the forehead. No matter how rough things got between them, whenever she was in Karl's arms, she felt as though she was right where she belonged.

A huge part of Bonnie needed to know why he did what he did. Karl was big on not addressing his mistakes. He always expected Bonnie to just forget, and move on. She kept a lot of things bottled up when it came to her feelings, but not this time.

"Karl I just want you to know what you did hurt me so bad," she said. 'I can't believe that you brought someone into our home and in our bed."

"I know baby. I fucked up. I wasn't thinking clearly. She meant nothing to me. I just met her that night," he said.

"That's even worse. Why would you bring a chick that you barely know to our house? Don't you know she could've set you up? I thought you knew better than that."

"You're right. And I'm sorry. I will never disrespect you like that again," he said.

"You're right…cause I won't let you. And this bed. I will

not sleep on this fucking bed Karl. Throw this shit out," she said, while pointing her finger at him.

"Done," he said. "Matter of fact, we need a fresh start anyway. I want you to start looking for a new place."

"Sounds good to me," she said.

Bonnie loved the idea of having a fresh start with Karl. There were already too many bad memories in that house. Besides, too many people knew where they lived and it made her uncomfortable. She always told Karl he shouldn't let so many people know where they lived. He never listened though. Karl wasn't the loner type, he kept a lot of company. It didn't matter if they were just workers, flunkies or whatever, they were all welcome in his home. Bonnie wasn't from the streets but she was wise enough to know this would soon be his downfall.

Two months later, Bonnie and Karl were settled into their new place. It was an 1150 sq. ft. two bedroom, two bath condo, located in Montgomery County. It had shiny hardwood floors, a huge living room and dining room, eat in kitchen, and a roof deck. It was perfect for starting a new family.

Bonnie thought since they moved away from the city, he would be more low key but she was wrong. He didn't know how to separate his life in the streets from his personal life, and this drove Bonnie crazy. She knew half of the guys Karl kept around him weren't cool. She could look in their eyes and tell they weren't genuine nor were they loyal.

Bonnie was now three months pregnant and finally over the morning sickness. She was so sick she could barely get out of bed and make it to class. She fell so far behind in school, she actually considered withdrawing from all of her classes but her professors allowed her to send in all of her assignments via email. Now she was back on campus, on track and getting straight A's again. Just when she thought that everything was on the up and up, she got slapped in the face by Karl and his infidelity.

One night, Mehki was over to their house. He and Karl

had been bagging up coke and counting money. Bonnie was in her bedroom, lying in bed and watching TV. Karl came into the bedroom to check on Bonnie. "Hey baby, you good? he said. "Yeah, I'm just tired," she replied. Karl told her he had to make a run but, he'd be right back. He placed his cell phone on the dresser and started looking for something to change into. Karl left out of the bedroom, and unintentionally left his phone on the dresser.

Bonnie heard a constant vibrating noise, and realized that it was Karl's phone. She got out of bed, picked up his phone, and saw the name Monica flashing across the screen.

"Hello," Bonnie said. There was complete silence on the other end of the phone, and then the call ended. *I know this bitch ain't just hang up on me*, Bonnie said to herself. She called the number back.

"Why you hang up? You calling for Karl right?" Bonnie said, with an attitude.

"Listen, I'm not trying to get into this shit with you," she said. "You and I both know what's up."

"No I don't sweetie," she said, sarcastically. "You tell me what's up. Why are you calling my man?"

"Why don't you ask your man?" she replied.

"I'm asking you because these niggas lie. Now woman to woman, talk to me."

Monica paused for a moment, before she gave Bonnie a response.

"Well, I've been messing with Karl for about two and a half months and I'm not mad at you for what you did to me that day," she said. "As a woman I understand how you must've felt."

"What are you talking about?" Bonnie asked.

"That morning, when you jumped on me," she said.

"Wait a minute. Hold up. You're the girl, that was in my house?"

"Yeah. I thought you knew," she said. Bonnie's heart dropped to the floor.

"You got the nerve to say you understand how I must've

felt, but you still fucking my man bitch. You better pray I don't ever run into you, because I'ma fuck you up again," Bonnie, spat.

Karl heard Bonnie yelling, and he rushed into the room. When he saw Bonnie holding his phone, he already knew what it was hitting for. He snatched the phone out of Bonnie's hand, and saw that it was Monica. He immediately hung the phone hung up and was heated.

"You still fucking that bitch Karl? What is wrong with you?" she screamed at him.

"Why you always gotta go looking for shit?" You allow your insecurities to fuck us up every time," he said.

"You can't be serious. The bitch kept calling your phone. I didn't go looking for shit!" she screamed. "Is she the reason why we haven't fucked in almost a month?"

"I'm not fucking that girl. We just talked on the phone a few times, that's it," he said, lying through his teeth.

Karl hadn't been interested in having sex with Bonnie at all. This really messed with her head because she knew how much he liked to have sex. Monique told her it was because she was pregnant, and he believed it would hurt the baby. Bonnie knew her man, and she felt as though something was up…she knew he was getting it elsewhere.

"Karl nothing is ever going to be enough for you. No matter how much I try to love you, it's never enough. I wish I never fucking met your lying ass. You ain't shit!" she said, meaning every single word.

Karl balled up his fist, punched Bonnie in the face, causing her to drop to the floor. She put her hands over her face, to block his punches, but he was still swinging and yelling at the same time.

"You're always looking for shit bitch! You bring out the fucking worst in me!" Blood was pouring from Bonnie's mouth. Mehki came in and tried to pull Karl off of Bonnie, but he was unsuccessful.

"Yo! Karl, she's pregnant! Get off of her!" Mehki said.

"I don't give a fuck! I'm sick of this bitch!" he said, in a very angry voice.

Bonnie laid there in the fetal position, whimpering and begging Karl to stop. Hearing Bonnie's cries, made him snap out of the crazy rage that he was in. He eventually composed himself and stopped hitting her. Mehki was a ruthless, and reckless killer, but even he would've never hit a woman like that. Seeing Karl put his hands on Bonnie, the woman that was carrying his child, made him see Karl differently.

"Come on! let's get the fuck outta here!" Karl said to Mehki. He grabbed his keys off the dresser and left out of the bedroom, leaving Bonnie lying there on the floor.

"You alright Bonnie?" Mehki asked, while picking her up off the floor.

"Yeah I'm okay," she said, but it was clear she wasn't. She had a busted lip and her left eye was half shut.

"You're too pretty to let a nigga treat you like this Bonnie. For real. That shit ain't cool," he said. All of Karl's friends loved Bonnie, especially Mehki. She was a real sweetheart and a good person. They all felt as though she didn't deserve to be treated so badly by Karl.

"I know," she replied. "Thanks Mehki."

After they left, Bonnie went into the bathroom to clean herself up. She stared at herself in the mirror and didn't like the reflection looking back at her. Seeing what Karl did to her face made her angry but still loving him made her even more angry with herself.

Karl didn't come back that night. He returned the next morning with a pair of Chanel sunglasses, so she could hide her black eye, while she was in class. And just like all the other times he apologized, but still gave her bullshit reasons for why he did what he did. She couldn't tell any of her friends or family about what he'd done, especially not her father. She knew Michael would've killed Karl with his bare hands. She still needed to talk to someone about it, so she confided in Karl's mother, Ms. Lynn. She found great comfort in talking to his mother and also found the underlying issue to Karl's abusive behavior.

She told Bonnie Karl's father was abusive to her and the children as well. She also said, out of all the children, Karl seemed to get it worse than the others. He acted as though he hated him and he went out of his way to make Karl's life a living hell when he was a child. Karl had a lot of hurt and anger pent up inside of him that stemmed from his childhood.

Two nights later, Bonnie was home alone and lying in bed. She was feeling down and severely depressed because of everything she was going through with Karl. She began to feel sharp pains shooting in her lower stomach. The pain was excruciating and she knew something was terribly wrong. She got out of bed and walked to the bathroom, hunched over and holding her stomach. She pulled her pants out in front of her and saw that her panties were filled with blood.

She ran some bath water, and then grabbed her cell phone so she could call someone to take her to the hospital. She called Karl and he didn't answer. She tried him a few more times, but still he didn't answer. She sat in warm bath water to ease the intense cramps, and then called Monique.

"Hey girl. What's up."

"Mo, you busy?" she said. Monique could hear in Bonnie's voice that something was wrong.

"No. What's going on? Are you okay?" she asked.

"No I'm having a miscarriage," she said. I'm in so much pain girl. I'm sitting in the bath tub, and there's blood everywhere."

"Oh my gosh Bonnie! Okay, let me think…get out of the tub, you can get an infection like that. Now, try and stay calm, I'm on my way!"

Monique drove Bonnie to Abington Memorial Hospital. They took her straight to triage and then immediately assigned her to a room. After examining her, the doctors informed her she lost the baby, and it appeared everything expelled on its own. She was told miscarriages were very common in women who were still in their first trimester. Bonnie was discharged and told to follow up with her

OBGYN in three days.

Monique kept asking her if she was okay, but she was unsure herself about how she really felt. A part of her was sad she lost the baby, but then another part of her felt relieved. Karl was now revealing his true colors, and she felt deep down in her heart having a baby with him would've been a huge mistake. And one she would regret for years to come.

After Bonnie lost the baby, you would think it would've hit home with Karl, and opened his eyes to all of his wrong doing. Did he not see the role he was playing in Bonnie's life? Did he not understand the negative impact he would have on such an innocent young girl? And did he not know there would be consequences?

Things between the two of them spiraled completely out of control. They were at a point where they were fighting about something every other day. He got so comfortable with putting his hands on her, that he would hit her for no reason at all. He brought all of his problems from the outside, into their home, and if he was having a bad day, Bonnie would have to pay the price.

It was mid-May, when Bonnie concocted a plan for herself. She was over Karl and wanted nothing more than to be done with him. She was already placed on academic probation for failing all of her classes. And at this point, Bonnie could care less about school. She just needed to get herself together mentally. She developed low self-esteem and began viewing herself as unworthy and unlovable. Karl brought her down to such a low point. She felt like he sucked the life out of her and she had nothing left to give...not even to herself.

"Hey mom. I need to get away for a while. Can I come down there?"

"Of course you can. Is everything okay."

"No mom, it's not. I can't take Karl anymore and I just need to get out of here."

"Okay. So, when are you going to book your flight?"

"I'm driving. I'm going to pack my things into my car,

and just be out."

"Okay. Is Karl going to give you some money, before you leave?"

"He doesn't even know I'm leaving. He has about forty-thousand in our closet, and more in the basement. How much do you think I should take?" she said.

"Hell, take all of it." she replied.

"Mom, I can't do that. I'll take five thousand. That'll be enough to hold me over til' I get situated."

Karen snickered, "You're better than me, cause I damn sure would be taking more than five thousand."

"Of course you would mom," she said, sarcastically. "I'll call you tomorrow night, while I'm on the road. I love you."

"Love you too. Bye."

Karl's constant disrespect and disregard for Bonnie's feelings made it easy for her to go through with her plans the following night. She waited till around 8 o'clock, and called his phone to make sure he was still out and about. She packed all of her things, cleaned out her dresser drawers and left nothing but a Dear John letter.

Bonnie hopped on Highway 95 South, and was on her way to Georgia. She drove for about six hours straight, and then Karl started calling her phone nonstop. Bonnie pulled over at a Days Inn hotel, and got a room. She needed to get some rest, and she also wanted to think about whether or not she wanted to leave with Karl's money.

When she got into her room, she listened to all of Karl's messages. Surprisingly, he didn't sound angry. Bonnie called her mother in hopes that she could help her put things into perspective.

"Mom, I don't know what to do. Karl is calling my phone back to back," she said. "I just pulled over and got a room."

"How far are you?" Karen asked.

"I'm in Virginia. I'm thinking about just going back. I don't feel right leaving with his money."

"Don't you think he's already pissed off? He might try

and start some shit with you, if you go back?"

"I'm not going back to him. I just want to get his money back to him somehow. I'll figure it out mom."

"Okay. I love you. Call me when you get back to Philly."

"Alright. I love you too."

Bonnie took a deep breath, and built up the courage to call Karl. Just when she was dialing his number, Ms. Lynn's call came in. She asked Bonnie if she was okay, and told her Karl wanted her to come home. She said he wasn't upset and he blamed himself for everything. Whenever they had their spats he would always get his mom to call Bonnie and smooth things over.

"Hey," she said, in a low and pitiful voice.

"Where you at? I was worried about you," Karl said.

"I'm at a hotel," she said. "I'm sorry for taking your money."

"It's all my fault. I pushed you to this," he said, with sincerity. "I was on my way home to talk to you. I just wanted to make things right. I came home, and you were gone. It really fucked me up."

"So, you're not mad?" she asked.

"Naw. Out of all the money I had in the house, you only took three grand. That shows what type of person you are, cause a slimy bitch would've took all that shit."

Karl was off about the amount that she'd taken, and she didn't correct him either.

"I'm gonna send it back to you through Western Union."

"Bonnie, I'm not gon' touch you. I promise you," he said. "Can you just come home?"

She didn't go home that night. She stayed at the hotel, and in the morning she sent the money to Karl through Western Union, like she said she would. When she got back to Philly, she went to Monique' house. She told Monique about everything she'd been going through. Monique said to her, "Damn bitch, I can't believe you was just gon' leave and not tell us," she said. "And then your ass only took five thousand. If you gon' leave you supposed to take all that shit." Bonnie just shook her head and laughed.

Bonnie stayed with Monique for a couple days, before giving in to Karl and going home. Bonnie told herself *Just give it one last shot and if he fucks up again, be done with his ass for good!* This time she wasn't taking anymore of Karl's shit.

It was a hot summer night, and Art was fighting at the Asylum Arena in South Philly. He was going against some cat from Atlantic City, NJ. The entire city had been talking about this fight. Monique, Tess, and Bonnie were dressed to kill that night, and they knew all eyes would be on them. It had been a while since the three of them hung out together, and they planned on going hard that night.

Art scored a knockout in the fifth round. He and his friends were going to 8th Street Lounge to celebrate and they invited the girls to come along. Tess's brother gave her some weed and she brought it along for the ride. They all shared a blunt, before they got to the club, and it had them feeling like they were on cloud nine. At that moment, Bonnie didn't have a care in the world. She felt free and her mind was at ease.

When they got to the club, they spotted Art and his friends in VIP. They motioned for the girls to come over. They were popping bottles of Cristal and partying like it would be there last. Bonnie, Tess, and Monique walked over to their table, already hype and dancing. "Ahh shit!" Monique screamed out, while shaking her ass to R. Kelly and Jay Z's "Somebody's Girl." The three of them danced real close, sexy and seductively, putting on a show.

Karl texted Bonnie all night, telling her to hurry up and come home. She didn't drive her car that night, so she couldn't just up and leave. Besides, she was enjoying herself way too much. Everyone was going to Club Deco, an after hour spot on Spring Garden St. While they were leaving out and heading to their car, Bonnie spotted Karl's Mercedes Benz parked in front of the club. "I'm out ya'll, have fun and be safe." She hugged her girls goodbye, then got into the car with Karl.

"Every time you get with those smut ass bitches, you be on some bullshit."

"C'mon Karl. Not tonight."

"Fuck you mean not tonight! I told you not to go out in the first place!"

"I can go out if I want. You don't own me," she said. "That's the problem, you think you do."

"Bitch I made you. When I met you, you ain't have shit," he spat. "Look at this shit...six hundred dollar dress, Gucci bag, Monolo Blahniks. You wasn't rocking this shit before me."

"You're right. I didn't have all of this but at least I was happy. I didn't have to deal with your nut ass!" she said, raising her voice.

Before Bonnie could even blink, Karl's fist smashed her in the eye. He was wearing two diamond rings on his finger, which made a deep cut underneath her eyebrow. She put her hand over her eye and blood started gushing through her fingers. "Oh no you didn't muthafucka!" she screamed. Bonnie reached over the seat and punched him in the face. Bonnie's blow caught Karl completely off guard. He wasn't used to her fighting back. She then stretched her body across the arm rest and bit him on the chest. "Ahh fuck! You crazy bitch!" For a moment, he lost control of the wheel and Bonnie swung again. "Fuck you pussy! You make me crazy! I'm sick of you putting your hands on me!" The car swerved, as they fought on the expressway like two crazy people.

When they got home the fight only escalated. Bonnie was the one that edged things on this time. She thought about everything that Karl put her through over the years. She had visuals of him cheating, all the lies, and every time he laid his hands on her. There was so much adrenaline pumping through her veins that she couldn't control herself. "This is what you want! You don't like the sweet, good girl, huh pussy!" she yelled. Karl took things to a whole new level, when he pulled out a gun and put it to Bonnie's head. "I should blow your mutherfuckin head off," he said, with a menacing scowl on his face. "I dare you…do it," she said, while staring in his eyes. He stared back at her and replied, "If I thought I could get away with it, I would." And right then and there, she knew she had to get away from him. The crazy thing is when he put the gun to her head, she didn't feel an ounce of fear. She didn't know if he would really pull the trigger or not, but there was one thing she did know…it was time to bring an end to this crazy, and dangerous love affair.

CHAPTER SEVEN
I Just Want It to Be Over

Karen Summers anxiously waited for her daughter outside of Delta Baggage Claim, at the Hartsfield-Jackson Atlanta Airport. She stood there leaning against her Cadillac Escalade, while all the men were gawking at her. She was wearing a tank top and cut off jean shorts, showing off her thick, toned legs. Karen sure was a piece of work. Now at thirty-seven years old, she gave most twenty year olds a run for their money. She was still doing her thing too. Karen had a nice house in Stone Mountain, GA, two cars that were paid for, and a closet full of designer clothes and shoes. Although Karen was making a pretty good salary as a nurse, she still enjoyed milking players for everything they had.

"Bonnie! Look at you, you're so pretty!" she said, excitedly.

"Thanks mom, and so are you!" she said, while wrapping her arms around her.

"I'm so glad you're here, we're going to have so much fun!" Karen said.

"Mom, is that your truck?" she said, while checking out the twenty-inch custom rims.

"Of course it is…you know how I do," she replied, laughing. Karen grabbed Bonnie's luggage and put it in the trunk. She was so happy to be with her daughter, she couldn't stop smiling. It was a good feeling to have her daughter sitting on the passenger side, while she drove. It was just like the old days.

"Mom I found a place that doesn't require an entertainer's license," she said. "It's called Showgirls Cabaret and it's in Athens. Have you ever heard of it?"

"No I haven't heard of that one, but we can go check it out. Are you sure you really want to do this? I'll give you the money, so that you can get your own place."

"Mom, I don't want to take your money. I'll get it myself. Besides, I won't have to work there long. I'm only gon' do it for two weeks."

"Okay. You know I'm backing you regardless," she said.

"I know that," Bonnie said, with a warm smile on her face.

Bonnie was determined to get her own money. She felt as though she had something to prove to Karl. She wanted to show him she didn't need him and she could make it on her own. After their last fight she packed all of her things, and took most of it to Monique's house. Karl started hiding his money from Bonnie, since the time she took a few thousand and left. So she called his mother for some light cash. She gave Bonnie four hundred dollars out of Karl's stash, so she could purchase a plane ticket.

Bonnie decided she was going to dance at a strip club for a couple of weeks, just to get enough money to get her own apartment, in Philly. She already found a cute one bedroom apartment in Germantown, and it was only five hundred dollars a month. The owner wanted first month, last month and security, but she liked Bonnie so much; she told her to give her a thousand, and the place was all hers.

Karen and Bonnie didn't waste any time. The next afternoon, they drove an hour to Athens to check out Show Girls Cabaret. The club was a very nice and classy spot. The girls on the other hand, weren't so classy. Most of them looked ratchet, and worn out. As soon as they walked to the bar they were greeted by the owners, Bill and Samantha. They were husband and wife, and Samantha was also a dancer at the club. They looked Bonnie up and down, and knew she would be an instant hit at their club. Although, all of the dancers were black, none of them were physically on Bonnie's level.

"How old are you?" Samantha asked.

"Nineteen. I'll be twenty in August," she said.

"What name are you going by?"

"Heaven."

"That fits you perfectly. You can start tomorrow night. Be sure to bring your ID with you, so I can make a copy for our records."

"Okay. Thank you so much. See you tomorrow night."

Now all Bonnie had to do was buy some exotic wear to dance in. Karen drove her to a boutique, in downtown Atlanta. She didn't know exactly what was stripper appropriate. She just bought a lot of sexy G-strings and lingerie tops. She never imagined she would be out shopping for stripper clothes with her mom, let alone working in a strip club, but Bonnie was ready to get that paper.

The next night, Bonnie nervously walked into Show Girls, nowhere near ready to take on a crowd of thirsty men. She was escorted to the girls changing room by the club's house mom. Bonnie felt so awkward and out of place, but did an incredible job disguising it. All of the girls were changing into their clothes, putting on makeup and doing their hair. When Bonnie saw their outfits, she was ashamed to even pull out her so called stripper attire. These chicks had glow in the dark thongs and pants, sexy gowns, and sparkly high stripper heels, and boots. All of them had long weaves down their back, and an exotic look about them. And here was Bonnie with her hair pulled back in a bun, looking as sweet and innocent as can be.

"What's your name boo?"

"Heaven."

"I'm Secret," she said. "You're so pretty. Where you from?"

"I'm from Georgia, but I live in Philly now. Been there for about seven years."

"Oh okay. You work in a club before?" she asked.

"Yeah. I've been dancing on and off for about a year," Bonnie said, lying. She didn't want any of the girls knowing it was her first time dancing in a strip club. She thought they would try her if they knew she was new to the game.

"That's wassup. Just to give you a heads up, don't trust none of these hoes in here. They all a bunch of shady, jealous bitches."

"I'm not worried about these bitches," Bonnie said. "I'm not here to make friends. I'm just tryna get my money."

"I know that's right!" Secret said, while giving Bonnie a high five. Secret was tall, brown skinned and wasn't the most attractive female, but she had a lot of sex appeal. She was very thick, with a big ass, small waist, and flat stomach. She'd been dancing since she was sixteen years old. Now at twenty-seven, she was definitely a veteran in the game.

Bonnie changed into a red G-string, and a red lace mini dress. She wore black, tie up platform heels that weren't the traditional stripper shoe, but were still very sexy heels. She walked over to the DJ booth and gave the DJ a list of songs to play for her. She stood next to the booth and waited for a dancer to finish up her routine. As the other dancer collected her money and left the stage, Bonnie could feel her throat knotting up.

"Alright you guys, we have a special treat for you tonight. Something hot, something fresh, sexy and beautiful! Everyone…welcome Heaven to the stage."

The crowd started cheering Bonnie on, and they were loving her the moment she stepped out on the floor. She was nervous at first, but once she walked onto that stage, and heard her song blasting through the speakers, she swallowed all her fears and was ready to get it popping! "You're contagious, touch me baby, give me what you got. Sexy lady drive me crazy, drive me wild…" Bonnie seductively walked to the middle of the stage, and slid her back down the pole, spreading her legs wide open. She moved her body in a circular motion, while lip synching the words to "Contagious" by the Isley Brothers. She had everyone's attention, and they instantly started throwing money on the stage. The way that Bonnie was working it, you would've never believed that it was her first night as a dancer.

Usually each girl would dance for only two songs but the crowd was feeling Bonnie so much, the DJ signaled Bonnie to stay on. The very thing that Bonnie was self-conscious about is what the guys loved most about her. She kept hearing all night how refreshing it was to finally see a girl who wasn't dressed like everyone else. They liked that she didn't dance in stripper clothes and that she had more of a girl next door look.

Bonnie didn't have to press hard to get her dances. They were approaching her left and right for private lap dances. When she got her first dance, she walked into the private room, and saw Secret grinding hard on some guy. Bonnie didn't know she was supposed to wait until Secret finished. She walked in and sat on the sofa next to her and started to strip out of her clothes.

Secret stood up, cut her eyes at Bonnie, and abruptly left the room.

"Oh my gosh. You're so beautiful," the nerdy, white man said. Bonnie could feel him getting rock hard though his pants, as she straddled him.

"Thank you," she said.

"Can I touch it please…I just want to smell it," he said, revealing his perverted side.

"No, you can't touch it. But if you give me an extra hundred dollars, I'll let you see it."

"Okay," he said, eagerly. He handed Bonnie a crisp hundred dollar bill and she pulled her G-string to the side so he could catch a quick glimpse.

"It's nice and bald," he said, while licking his lips. "I bet it taste so good" *I wish this song hurry up and go off so I can be done with this nasty fuck* she thought to herself. Bonnie gave him a quick smile, trying to hide her annoyance. She finished her lap dance and on her way out of the private room, Secret was standing off to the side waiting for her.

"You worked in a club before right?" she asked, with an irked expression on her face.

"Yeah. What's up?" she asked.

"I was giving a private dance and you just barged in there like you ain't see me doing my thing."

"My bad. I didn't know there was only one girl allowed in at a time. You should've said something."

"Well, I just thought you knew the rules," she said, sarcastically.

Bonnie snapped back. "Well I didn't! And don't keep going on and on about the shit. I said my bad, now excuse me I got money to make."

She gave Secret a look that let her know she wasn't the one, and then brushed past her, purposely bumping her shoulder. Secret was used to running Show Girls and being the most desired, but Bonnie had come in and took over that night. She couldn't stand it one bit but Bonnie was never the type of girl to get intimidated by anyone. She was going to do her regardless. Funny how Secret warned Bonnie about jealous, shady bitches...she should've been wearing a warning sign on her forehead.

That night, Bonnie had the biggest pay out to the club, which meant she made the most money. Her first night, she walked out of the club with a little over nine hundred dollars. She couldn't believe she made so much money in one night. She realized she wouldn't have to be there for more than a week. It wasn't like she enjoyed stripping. She could never see herself getting caught up in that lifestyle. She had a plan and she was sticking to it.

When Bonnie got to her mother's she took a long hot bath. She soaked in the tub for at least an hour, while reflecting on everything leading up to this night. She thought about Karl and what they once had. When they first got together he was like a breath of fresh air. She never thought she could love a man so deeply. And after everything they'd been through, she still loved him but she was finally realizing like oil and water, they didn't mix.

Over the next few days, Bonnie was focused. She went to work faithfully, with the intent to make at least five hundred a night. She met a not so attractive, white truck driver, by the name of Dean. He was from Denver, Colorado, recently divorced, and had bad luck when it came to women. After only two lap dances, Bonnie knew his entire life story. He told her he'd been married twice to women half his age, and they both took advantage of him financially. He was vulnerable and desperately looking for someone to love him. When he saw Bonnie it was love at first sight. Well, lust at first sight might be a better choice of words.

Dean hated seeing her go in the back to give private dances. He tried his best to keep her occupied for most of the night. Bonnie didn't mind at all, because she made a lot of money off of him and it was easy money. She would sit in the VIP lounge with him for hours, talking about his problems, while sipping on champagne.

It was a Friday night, and the house was packed. There were a couple of players from the Atlanta Falcons, and they were all showing mad love. Bonnie took the stage and shut it down just like any other night. She didn't know how to work that pole but she sure knew how to move her body and bounce her ass. "Baby grind on me. Relax your mind, take your time with me. Let me get deeper shorty ride on me. Now come and sex me till your body gets weak. Just grind with me baby…" Bonnie crawled on her knees, licking her lips, and playing on the crowd. Her signature move that drove the men crazy, was when she laid on her back, with both legs in the air, shaking them and making her ass clap.

By the end of the night, Bonnie had made eleven hundred dollars. It was the most that she'd ever made in a single night. Before she went into the dressing room to change out of her clothes, the club DJ approached her.

"Here Heaven, this is from Bill."

"Bill who?" The owner Bill?" Bonnie asked, with one eyebrow raised.

"Yeah. He wanted me to give this to you," he replied. "He said, it's because you did such a great job on stage."

"Okay. Well, tell him I said thanks," she said. She turned her back towards everyone, so she could count the money without anyone noticing. Bill gave her two hundred dollars. Bonnie knew he gave her the money for a reason. He was trying to ease his way in. *Damn, men ain't shit* she thought to herself. *This fool tryna play right in front of his wife.*

Bonnie was leaving an hour early before the club closed. She was happy with the amount of money she made and was just ready to get out of there and hit the highway. When she walked into the dressing room, all of the chattering that Bonnie heard on the other end of the door instantly stopped. It was dead silence the moment she walked in. Bonnie just laughed to herself when she saw Secret and the other two dancers, sitting there and staring her down. Bonnie took her shoes off and then pulled her duffle bag out of the locker.

"Why you leaving so early?" Secret asked.

"Because I want to," she said, sneeringly.

"Oh, well excuse the fuck outta me," she said, while stroking her fingers through her long weave.

"Whatever," Bonnie said.

When Bonnie got finished changing into her clothes, Samantha came in to collect her house fee. Bonnie went to use the ladies room, which was in the same area as the dressing room, but only down the hall. She put her duffle bag in her locker but slipped up and forgot to lock it. When she returned and opened the locker, she noticed her bag was positioned differently, and then she quickly discovered her money bag was missing.

"Yo! Who touched my shit!?"

"What are you talking about?" Secret asked, with a smirk on her face.

"You bitches got me fucked up! I'm about to spaz out. Where is my fucking money!" she yelled. "Sage, Secret,

Butterfly…one of you bitches better start talking."

A shaken Sage, looked at Bonnie and hinted with her eyes that Secret had taken her money. Butterfly stepped to the side, and away from Secret, which was all the confirmation that Bonnie needed.

"Secret give me my money, or we gon' fight in this muthafucka!"

"Is that what you want Heaven? You wanna fight?" she replied, while snickering.

Bonnie hauled off and punched Secret in the face with all her strength. Secret fell against the locker and Bonnie just went in, landing one punch after another.

"You nut ass bitch! You fucked with the wrong one!" she said, right before kneeing her in the stomach. Secret straightened herself up and swung at Bonnie, finally landing a punch across her face. Bonnie recovered quickly and attacked her like she was trying to put her in the hospital. Even while Secret was on the floor, Bonnie was kicking her, digging her six inch heel into her face! "I will fucking kill you bitch!" Bonnie screamed.

Sage rushed out of the room to get security, while Butterfly just stood there. Bonnie rummaged through Secret's locker until she spotted her royal blue money bag, with all of her cash in it. "You thieving ass hoe," Bonnie said. She kicked Secret again, grabbed her things and then left.

"Heaven what happened?" Are you okay? Bill asked.

"Naw, that trifling bitch Secret tried to steal from me. So, I whooped her ass. She's the one ya'll need to be checking on."

"This isn't the first time we've heard this. We just never had any proof. She's gone. She's outta here."

"No, she can stay. I'm out."

"You mean…you're not coming back?" he asked, with a confused look on his face.

"That's right. I'm not coming back," she said, as she turned away and left.

She planned on finishing out the weekend but with

everything that happened with Secret, she decided to cut her weekend short. Besides, she made more than enough money to go back home and move into her apartment. Her goal was to make at least three thousand but in six days she made forty-two hundred.

Bonnie went home and told her mom all about her fight at the club. The first thing she said was, "I'm glad you whooped her ass!" Bonnie laughed and replied, "Trust me, I whooped it good too! They laid in bed together like they used to when Bonnie was a little girl, just laughing and talking until one of them fell asleep.

"Mom, this is the guy Dean calling me now," she said, excitedly.

"Bonnie, I told you to hit his ass up for some money."

"I don't know mom," she said. "Here, you answer and pretend like you're me. We sound just alike anyway."

Karen had a Doctorates degree in mind fucking men and taking their money, so she was more than happy to see what she could squeeze out of Dean for her daughter.

"Hey Heaven."

"Hey Dean. It's funny that you called because I was just thinking about you."

"You were?" he asked, sounding as if he was blushing.

"Yup," she said, in a cute baby doll voice. "Dean I don't want to work in the club anymore."

"You shouldn't. You're too darn precious to be working as a stripper."

"I know. That's why I quit tonight. I hated working in that crummy ol' place anyway," Karen said, putting on her sad voice.

"Bonnie I told you if you move to Colorado with me I would take care of you. You wouldn't have to work. All you would have to do is be my wife."

"Aww you're so sweet. That's something that could definitely happen in the future, maybe after I finish school," she said, lying.

Karen told him she needed to be back in Philly to finish

school but he was more than welcome to visit her anytime. She also told him she only came to Georgia to escape a crazy, stalker ex-boyfriend. Karen told him she was dancing just to make enough money to get her own apartment, and to be able to furnish it. She was good at making men feel sorry for her, like they were her only hope. By the end of their phone conversation, he was telling Karen he would wire her two thousand dollars, the following morning.

"Mom are you serious?" she laughed. He's going to send two thousand dollars?

"Yup! He sure is. I told you I got you," she said, while smiling at Bonnie.

"Oh my God! Thanks mom! I have all I need now!" she said, smiling from ear to ear.

"Now you can go back to Philly, get your place, and be in your own shit."

"I know mom. I can finally get my life back on track," she said. "I can't wait to get back home."

CHAPTER EIGHT
You're all I Need To Get By

"Bonnie I love your apartment. I'm sooo jealous," Monique said.

"I know right! How does it feel to have your own space?" Tess asked.

"It feels good. I wouldn't trade it for nothing in the world," she said, while laughing.

"Whatever bitch. Don't be fronting like you don't miss Karl though," Monique teased.

"Naw. I'ma keep it one hundred with ya'll. I do miss him. I miss the shit outta him. But I don't miss all that extra shit. I'm tired of going back and forth with him. It's draining," she said.

"I feel you girl. I respect you for leaving and getting your own place."

"Thanks. That's the same thing his mom told me. She said not a lot of girls my age would've done that. But you know what. It just seems like when you let a nigga do everything for you, they start to think they own you."

"Girl you ain't never lied! I'm going through the same thing with Art," Monique said.

"Sometimes you have to show these niggas that you

don't need them. Then they'll be right back on your top again," Bonnie said, referring to her situation with Karl. Ever since he found out that Bonnie had her own place, he'd been on her like white on rice.

"C'mon ya'll let's go so we can catch the nine o'clock," Tess said.

"Tess I told you we're not going to see no damn Batman Begins. You go see that shit with Art," she said. "We're going to see Mr. and Mrs. Smith and it don't start till ten."

"See ya'll hoes don't never wanna go see the movies I like."

"Yeah, cause you like corny shit," Monique said. "Let's get outta here ya'll so we can eat first."

After the girls left Houlihan's restaurant on City Line Avenue, they went to the Bridge Movie theatre on 40th St. They intended on having a drama free girls night out, but when Monique spotted Art and some other red boned chick everything went south.

"Oh hell naw! Look at this nigga!" Monique said, angrily.

"Who?" Bonnie asked, while squinting her eyes to zoom in on their target.

"Art, with his lying ass!" she said, while walking fast paced in his direction.

Bonnie and Tess hurried behind her because they knew Monique was about to get at the chick he was with.

"Who the fuck is she?"

"Hey baby," he said, nervously.

"Don't hey baby me pussy. Who is this bitch?" Monique said, while pointing her finger in the girl's face.

"Nobody. She just a friend."

"Oh really?" she said, sarcastically. She then turned to the frightened chick he was with, "You fucking with him like that?"

"We just met," she said, with a crackling voice.

"I want to hit you so bad right now, but I know this nigga is the one to blame. So, you can just step the fuck off. I'ma let you slide."

Even though Monique was dead serious, Bonnie and Tess couldn't help but laugh after what she said to the girl. And she didn't waste any time getting the hell out of dodge either. She saw the crazy look in Monique's eyes and she didn't want any problems with her.

"C'mon Monique chill out," he said. "Aye yo, Bonnie get your girl!"

"I'ma let her grind your ass up," she said, while laughing. "You deserve it."

"I'ma catch up with ya'll later," Monique said, while gripping Art up.

"We already knew that was coming anyway. Be safe, and make sure you call us," Tess said. There was never a dull moment. It seemed as though there was always some drama surrounding the three of them.

Over the next few weeks, Bonnie spent a lot of time with Karl. He would come over to her house every day, and most of the time they would just sit and talk for hours. He confided in Bonnie about a lot of things that were bothering him. He told her he couldn't trust any of his homeboys anymore, not even Mehki. Word on the street was that Mehki was a snitch. Karl became so paranoid, that he would circle the block at least four times before parking and he'd been sleeping with his Ruger pistol under his pillow.

He didn't tell Bonnie exactly why he couldn't trust Mehki, but she already knew from the rumors. Karl never got Bonnie involved with his life on the other side of the game. The most she ever did was count his drug money but now he was having her involved in minor drop-offs, and sometimes if he was moving drugs from one place to another, he would have Bonnie closely trail him in her car, so there was no chance he'd be pulled over by the cops.

Karl told Bonnie he never stopped loving her but his lifestyle took a heavy toll on him mentally, which prevented him from treating her the way he was supposed to. He broke down in tears one night and apologized for everything he'd ever done wrong to her. He admitted to taken her love for granted and said he would do anything in his power to make it right. But unfortunately Karl wouldn't have the opportunity to repair what was so terribly broken.

It was July 22, 2005, when Bonnie received a phone call from Karl's mother telling her he'd been locked up. The police set up surveillance and after a couple of weeks, they had more than enough evidence to arrest him. He was picked up on the corner of 42nd St. down the bottom. Shortly after his arrest, the police raided his West Philly apartment, confiscating cocaine and crack cocaine, with a street value of ninety-eight thousand dollars. They also found forty-eight thousand dollars in cash, a fully loaded Hi Point 40-caliber semi-automatic handgun, and a Ruger Revolver pistol.

The moment Karl was picked up, he knew it was all over for him. He was charged with multiple drug and gun charges, and he was facing serious jail time. His biggest fear was that the feds would pick up his case, and that was the last thing he wanted. Fortunately, he had the best lawyer in the city of Philadelphia on his case. She was able to get a lot of his charges dropped, and Karl was sentenced to five to eight years in a state prison.

He was sent to SCI Graterford, only an hour away in Collegeville, Pa. Bonnie was dying to see Karl. It had been a while since they saw each other. The entire time he was in the county jail awaiting sentencing, she saw him every week up until he started having his hearings. Karl didn't want Bonnie to attend any of them and he begged her not to come to his sentencing. He told her that he didn't want her hearing all of the negative things they had to say about him, and he didn't want her to see him being sent to prison.

The truth was Karl didn't know how much time he would get. He was hearing he would get twenty plus years and he was worried out of his mind. All he kept thinking about was everything he'd done to Bonnie over the years. He did a lot of horrible things, and all he could say was, *there's no way she gon' ride for me...she gon' leave me.* Still, Karl tried his hardest to hold on to her in any way he could. He even lied to her about the time he received. Instead of a five to eight, he told her he was sentenced to only three to five years.

Bonnie was determined to be there for him. Everything that he'd done to her, she completely brushed under the rug. She put her feelings aside in order to be there for Karl. There was no way she was going to let him do his time alone.

The first visit was hard on the both of them. Being as though Karl was in the hole, they weren't allowed to have face to face visits. She had to wait for a guard to pick her up and drive her on the other side of the prison yard. Then she was escorted down a long hallway, where they would have their visits. They talked on a telephone, with a thick glass between them and it broke Bonnie's heart seeing him like that.

"Baby, how are you feeling?"

"I'll be feeling a lot better once I get the fuck outta here," he said.

"I can't believe they would put you in here because of something that happened so long ago."

"That nut ass nigga found out I was here and he ran to the warden and said his life was in danger."

Eight years ago, Karl did some time at Graterford and he'd gotten into a huge fight with a cat named Tariq. What started as a harmless game of basketball; ended up having disrespectful words being spat at one another, which led to a nasty brawl between Tariq and Karl, leaving Tariq with a broken nose and a fractured rib.

"Well, it's okay. You'll be transferred soon. And baby I want you to know, I'm gon' be right here. I got you! I promise you that!" Bonnie said, meaning every word.

"Yo, I love you so much for that. You being here right now lets me know that everything is gonna be alright," he said, with tears building up in his eyes.

"I love you too Karl. More than anything in this world. We're just going through a rough time right now, but we got this. It ain't nothing that we can't handle."

"You're right, we're gonna get through this. As long as I

got you, I'm cool," he said, with sadness in his eyes. "Once I get to Mahanoy, we gon' be good."

Things at Mahanoy were definitely much better. The one thing Bonnie hated was the distance. It was three hours away in Frackville, Pa, and way out in the boondocks. She didn't complain though. She was just happy that she would be finally able to feel his touch again.

Bonnie arrived at the prison bright and early on a Monday morning. Karl warned her that the guards were pretty strict and that they wouldn't let her in if she was dressed overly sexy, so she kept it simple. She wore a pair of black leggings and a long shirt to cover her behind. She signed in, received a key and was told to put her belongings in a locker.

She was sent to a small room, to be searched and then sent through the metal detector. They also had a device they used to scan your hands. It would detect whether or not you were in contact with any drugs within the last twenty four hours. When the guard picked up the phone and said, "Atkins HQ5277 has a visit" Bonnie smiled from the inside out. She couldn't wait to wrap her arms around him.

Bonnie anxiously sat in the waiting room until the guard called out for her. "Atkins!" he yelled out. The doors opened and Bonnie walked through and down a long hallway. She then had to wait for another guard to open the door to the visiting area. When she walked in she saw Karl standing there waiting for her, with a big smile on his face.

"Hey baby," he said, while he squeezed her tight. "You look so good."

"Thank you. I missed you so much. You have no idea."

"I missed you too baby. Did you get the tokens for the food?"

"Yup I got the tokens and I got four picture tickets," she said.

Even in his brown jump suit, Karl still looked good to her. His hair was freshly cut, and he still had that swagger about him she loved so much. They went to the vending machines to get their food, and then waited in line to use the microwaves. They found a seat way in the back, where they could be off to themselves.

"See that's why I love you so much," he said, while admiring her. "You're right here eating this jail food with your man."

"Of course I am," she said, and then kissed him on the cheek.

When the guard called out Karl's last name, Bonnie knew it was time for her to go, and it almost brought tears to both of their eyes. Five and a half hours passed, and Bonnie would've stayed out in that visiting room all night long if they would've allowed her to. Unfortunately for the both of them, the visiting room was at full capacity, and whoever came in early for a visit, was always the first to go.

"Next week don't get here until around ten," Karl said. "That way we can stay out here longer."

"Okay…I don't want to leave you," she said, in a sad tone.

"I know baby. But I'm gon' call you as soon as I get back there alright? Give me a kiss."

Bonnie and Karl hugged each other real tight and kissed each other intensely. That visit had done so much for the both of them. Bonnie left Karl feeling less stressed and more at ease that day. They both believed that their love would be able to stand the test of time. But of course, when you've done as much dirt as Karl, there is always something in the past that resurfaces and gets in the way.

The following Monday morning, Bonnie arrived at Mahanoy at 10 o'clock. When she pulled in the parking lot she noticed a couple of men in uniform standing out in the parking lot, searching the visitor's vehicles. One of them motioned for Bonnie to pull over and then walked over to her.

"Good Morning. I'm Sergeant Cryer and we're performing searches on all vehicles entering the prison today," he said. "May I see your driver's license and registration?"

Irritated, she handed him her driver's license and registration.

"What's the name and the PP number of the inmate you're here to see?"

"Karl Atkins. HQ5277."

"Step out of your vehicle, while we perform a quick search. We'll have you on your way in no time."

After Sergeant Cryer and another officer performed their search, they found a small amount of marijuana residue in the ash tray. Bonnie was baffled at how it could've gotten there. She only smoked a couple of times with Monique and Tess, but never in her car. She argued with them back and forth, and tried to talk her way into the prison that day. She cried when she was told she wouldn't be allowed on the prison grounds.

"How long will this suspension last?" she asked, with tears in her eyes.

"You'll receive a letter in the mail from the warden explaining in further detail," he said, showing no sympathy for her whatsoever.

Bonnie snatched the notice of suspension out of his hand, jumped in her car and sped off. While on the long stretch of Route 61, making her way back home, she saw the 570 number flashing across her caller id. She was certain once he found out what happened it would only put him in a negative frame of mind. And that's the last thing she wanted.

"Hello."

"You have a prepaid call from…Karl, an inmate at a state correctional institution at Mahanoy…" Bonnie took a deep breath as she listened to the recording and prompts. She was nervous about delivering the bad news.

"Baby you alright?" he asked, sounding concerned. "Where you at?"

"You won't believe this shit that happened," she said. "I was just there and they were searching cars and they found weed residue in the ash tray."

"Why was there weed in your car?"

"I havè no idea how it got there. You know I don't smoke," she said.

"Ah shit, it must've been Mehki. When you was in Atlanta, I let him hold the car a couple of times," he said, in a frustrated voice.

"For real? I haven't checked the ash tray in all these months," she said. "Fuck! This is the last thing we need right now."

"Calm down, baby. We'll be alright. They probably only gonna suspend you for about a month," he said, trying to stay positive.

Two weeks later, Bonnie received a letter in the mail from the warden stating her suspension would remain in effect for an entire six months. Bonnie and Karl were both devastated but she made a promise to him it wouldn't affect their relationship at all. She told him while on suspension, she would go out of her way to make sure he felt her in every way possible.

And she did just that. He called Bonnie twice a day, and she never missed a call. She wrote him letters every day, sent him magazines and took a lot of those nasty, freaky pictures he so often requested. She would either have Monique or Tess take the pictures for her and she would go all out with her lingerie and outfits too. You would think she was submitting her pictures to King Magazine or something, that's how serious she was about it.

Five months had gone by and Bonnie managed to get a good paying job. Even from jail, Karl was helping Bonnie tremendously with her bills. She didn't like taking money from him while he was locked up. During the raid the cops confiscated all of his money in the apartment but he kept an emergency stash at his mother's. Still, Bonnie wanted to help him stack and not blow the twenty something thousand he had left to his name.

Now that she had her new job at Healthy System, as a weight loss counselor, she was good. She was making enough money to cover all of her bills, and she was able to put money on his books from time to time. And even though he told her not to, she would send him money orders to buy time on the phone. She wanted to show him she was able to hold him down. But Just when things were looking up for the both of them, they took a turn for the worse.

One night, Bonnie was at a Hess gas station on Broad and Stenton. She ran in to pay for her gas but left her car running, while she went inside. She came outside and saw a young guy wearing a black hoodie, hop into her car and pull off. She ran after him and into the intersection. A stranger that was pumping his gas, pulled off and chased him down Broad street but he lost him in all the traffic.

"Dammit!" Bonnie screamed out. "When it rains, it fucking pours," she said to herself. Since Tess only lived a couple of blocks away she called her to come get her. She went to the police station, to file a police report and then Tess drove her home. She was drained from the whole mess. It seemed like there was always some shit happening to get in the way, especially when she felt like she had a grip on things.

Later that night when Karl called Bonnie, he didn't stay on the phone long with her. After she told him what happened, he said he would make some calls to arrange a car for her to get around in. When Bonnie hung up the phone all she kept thinking was *why the hell does he need to call around for…where is his damn Benz?* She couldn't wait for him to call her back.

"Call Ted, he gon' let you drive one of his cars for a week or so, until I can get you the Benz."

"What do you mean until you can get it? You said it's parked at your sister's house right?" she asked.

"Chill out Bonnie. I'm tryna make sure you can get back and forth to work."

"And I appreciate that, but you haven't answered my question. Your car is at your sister's right?"

"Yes baby. I'll have it to you by the end of the week," he said. "Don't worry I'll take care of it."

Ted gave Bonnie a Cadillac DTS to drive for the week, and by Friday Karl told Bonnie she could go by his mother's house, and get the Benz. When she got there his mother handed her over the keys and registration. She told Bonnie his sister lost the title and she was going to have another one sent by Penndot.

"Hey baby. Did you get the car?" Karl asked.

"Yeah, I got it. I'm just leaving your mom's now," she said. "Who is Michelle Thompson?

"I don't know, why you ask that?" he said, lying through his teeth.

"That's the name on your registration," she said, in a confused voice.

"Oh it must be Felicia's girlfriend. I didn't know til' now she tried to sell my car. Supposedly her girlfriend didn't give her all the money for it so she took it back...I don't know, some shit like that," he said, digging a deeper grave for himself. Although the story didn't make sense to Bonnie, she still didn't expect foul play on Karl's end. He actually succeeded in making her believe he was just as confused as she was. She just wanted to get the car out of the woman's name and into hers. So, when Karl said they were having a hard time getting the title, Bonnie decided to go to the address listed on the registration.

Bonnie pulled up in front of the apartment building located on the corner of Belmont Avenue. She glanced at the registration again to check for the apartment number before going inside. The dreary hallway had a musty smell and wreaked of cigarette smoke. *Here it is 431...Knock Knock Knock.* She waited and then gave it a few more knocks. *Knock Knock Knock* But luckily for her there was no answer.

When she got in the car she called Karl's mother to see if they had any luck reaching this Michelle chick. "Hey Ms. Lynn, have you guys talked to her yet, cause I'm just leaving her house and no one answered the door," Bonnie said.

"You're leaving Michelle's house?" his mother asked, with worry in her voice.

"Yup. I need to get that title," she said.

"Oh, Lord Jesus. What is Karl doing?" The way those words uttered out of her mouth, it was clear she didn't mean to say them out loud.

"What do you mean?" Bonnie asked.

"Nothing, just let me work things out on my end okay. You don't need to go back over there. I'll take care of it," she said. At this point, Bonnie knew something was going on. She just didn't know what.

A few days later, she received a message on Myspace from an anonymous person named Zoey. It was clear to Bonnie it wasn't a real name nor was it a real page, because there was no profile picture. She asked Bonnie if her boyfriend's name was Karl. "Zoey" wrote she never forgets a face and she remembers seeing them out together a lot. In spite of the name and fake page, Bonnie responded back anyway confirming she was Karl's girlfriend.

Bonnie's cell phone started ringing and she knew it was Karl. It was 8:30 on the dot and Karl was never a minute late with his phone calls.

"Hey baby!" she said, ecstatically.

"Wassup," he said. "Why does your Myspace page say that you're single and what's up with all these nut ass freaky pictures you got on your page?"

"First of all, if it says single I never paid any attention to it. It's automatically set by default and as far as freaky pictures, I don't know what the hell you're talking about," she spat.

"Somebody printed out your page and mailed it to me," he said.

"Some bitch named Zoey messaged me and asked me if you were my boyfriend. I should've known she was up to some shit. So who is the bitch that sent it to you?"

Karl recognized he was digging a hole for himself and he quickly tried to change the subject.

"I don't know who it was. The name on the envelope was John Miller. It's just one of them hating ass bitches tryna come between us, that's all. Fuck em baby."

While Karl was trying to get Bonnie's mind off of everything he'd just told her, Bonnie was already on her computer messaging "Zoey" back. She wrote a vicious note to her and it was enough to piss the girl off so much, she revealed everything. She responded back to Bonnie in less than twenty minutes.

Little girl nobody's hating on you and Karl's relationship. I just didn't think he would have wifed up such a little whore but I should've known better because he's nothing but a whore himself. You can have him right now. He's your headache but when he comes home I'm going to continue fucking him because his dick is so long and thick just the way I like it. Oh and you can have that fucking Benz, I'm done with it! And tell your "man" I'll have the title for him soon.

Now it all made sense. The comment his mother made over the phone, having such a hard time getting the title, and that lame ass lie Karl told her about his sister selling the car. Bonnie was heated and she couldn't sleep the entire night. It drove her crazy she couldn't just call him and go off on him, or get in his face the way she needed to right at that moment.

When Karl called her the next morning, she couldn't wait to let him have it. She paced the living room floor, waiting for their call to be connected.

"You're a fucking liar Karl! And I'm so sick of your shit!" she screamed.

"What did I do?"

"I'ma give you a chance to come clean about the shit. Is the girl that contacted me on Myspace the same girl that had your car?"

"Yes. It's the same girl. Her name is Michelle," he said, in a low and pitiful voice.

"All this time I been on suspension that bitch was coming to see you. I saw the tokens in the car. I feel so stupid" she said. "I can't believe you gave her your car. Do you love her?"

"Hell no I don't love her and that's the truth. I never gave her my car, she was only keeping it for me. I didn't know she was putting the car in her name and all that."

"But she was coming to see you right?" she asked, even though she already knew the answer.

"Yeah she came up to see me a few times," he said.

"Wow. Here it is I'm breaking my back to make sure you're okay since I can't come see you but the whole time you getting visits from other bitches."

"Bonnie please just give me a chance to explain myself in person. This phone is about to cut off. You're off suspension next week, can you please just come see me."

"What's that bitch address?" she asked, ignoring his question. "Does she still live at the address that's on the registration?"

"Naw. It's 3624 Poplar St," he replied, without hesitation. "Will you come to see me next week?"

"Yeah. I'll be up there," she said.

"Alright I love you."

"Whatever Karl," she said, and then hung up the phone even before their one minute was up.

Bonnie changed into a sweat suit and a pair of sneakers. She put her hair in a ponytail and then wrapped a scarf around her head. She called her girls up and said, "Yo get dress, we're about to pay that bitch Michelle a visit." And like always Monique and Tess had her back. Bonnie picked up Tess first, and then they drove to Monique's. Bonnie left her car parked on Monique's block and they took her car. Bonnie didn't want Michelle to look out the window, recognize the Benz and then be afraid to open to the door.

"Alright ya'll stay right here unless you see some bitches try and roll on me. I don't know who she got in there so just be on point," she said, as she got out of the car.

She knocked on the door a few times and a young woman's voice called out. "Who is it?"

Bonnie didn't know what the hell to say. The first name that came to mind was Felicia. And it worked. A young light skinned girl opened the door, and immediately it dawned on Bonnie this was the same chick that was texting and sending pictures to Karl years ago. She yanked Michelle by her arm and pulled her further outside, so that she could give her a thorough ass whooping.

Bonnie started swinging, landing one punch after another on the girl's face. "You made a big mistake coming for me bitch!" Bonnie yelled out, before hitting her again. Monique and Tess saw a heavy set girl run outside and immediately started swinging on Bonnie. They both jumped out of the car and dived in on the action. Monique was wildin' out too, you would've thought Karl was her man. She was going way too hard on the both of them.

After giving both chicks a crazy beat down, they got the hell out of dodge fast before anyone called the cops. "Mo you was handlin' that big bitch!" Bonnie said, while laughing. "Shit all this built up anger inside of me. I saw every girl that Art ever cheated on me with, while I was out there swinging," Monique replied. They all laughed. To Bonnie, beating that girl's ass was like a weight being lifted off of her. Now she could go home and sleep like a baby.

The following week, Bonnie went to visit Karl but this visit would be nothing like the others. She didn't get any tokens for food, nor did she buy any picture tickets. She was sick off all the bullshit games and lies. She was only there to get everything off of her chest and check Karl's ass face to face.

"You wanted to talk to me so bad. So, talk," she said. "And I'm gon' tell you right now, don't start that lying shit cause I'll walk right out that fucking door!"

"I'm gon' be honest with you. After everything I put you through I thought you would leave me," he said. "I treated you so wrong when I was home."

"Yeah. But I thought we were passed all that. I told you that I wanted to be here for you."

"That's cause you love me. I never doubted your love for me but I thought eventually you would leave me. I was just using Michelle as something to fall back on. That's all," he said.

Bonnie didn't say a word, she just listened. "She knows how much I love you. I told her time and time again. And I promise to you she hasn't been up here to see me in months."

"Why is it that you never believe in me but yet you always want me to believe in you?" she asked.

"I do believe in you. I just know I did you wrong. The way you been holding me down all this time had me feeling so guilty," he said. "I was afraid I would lose you."

"Why did you treat me that way? You just don't know the damage you caused. You always made me feel like I wasn't good enough. There were times I felt like I ain't even want to live," she said, while looking down.

"I'm sorry baby. It's just that I was so deep in the streets, it fucked with my head. I was outta my mind half the damn time," he said. "I always loved you though. Ever since the first night I met you."

"Every time I think we're on a good note I get a slap in the face," she said, in a sad tone. "Just like when you got locked up, I didn't even know that you had another apartment in West Philly. I'm tired of being let down by you."

"I know and I'm sorry. I won't let you down again. Just give me a chance to come home and be a better man to you," he said. "That's all I want B."

"From this day forward no more lies. Either we in this together or not. There's no in between," she said. "I want you to remove Michelle and whoever else off your visiting list."

"Done. I been did that a while ago. And I'll send you the removal receipts in the mail so that you know I'm not bullshitting you. I don't need nobody else but you. Fuck all them chicks," he said, with sincerity. "You're all I need to get by."

CHAPTER NINE
Foolish

The following week, Bonnie went to visit Karl again. This visit went much smoother than the previous one. He sent her the removal receipts just like he promised, which gave Bonnie the security she needed. They vowed to never let anyone else come in between their relationship. All Karl wanted was the chance to come home so he could prove to Bonnie just how much he really did love her. For Karl, going to prison was a blessing in disguise. It sat him down and gave him a chance to think and see clearly without the distractions from the outside world. He missed his kids more than ever, and he wanted to be a better father. In a nutshell, he had a lot of making up to do with the people he loved the most.

At Mahanoy it was nothing but a big show in the visiting room. The guys would playfully argue back and forth about whose bitch was the baddest and they would place bets on whose chick would make it to the visiting room first. Of course, Karl loved to show off Bonnie's pictures. He knew he had the baddest young buck and the way she was riding for him made him just as cocky and confident in jail, as he was on the streets.

Bonnie spoiled him in there. She kept his mail flow heavy with letters, pictures, cards, magazines and street novels. She made sure she was there every Thursday morning at 8:30 sharp, and she was dressed to the nines. She always came in with a smile on her face, using her charm on the guards. She figured, if the guards liked her, they would give her special treatment. And she was right. The same correctional officers Karl labeled as racist dickheads sure loved seeing Bonnie's face on Thursdays. When she walked in and signed her name on the visiting list, they would automatically call down for Karl before she even passed through the metal detectors and security. She also didn't have to worry about being kicked out of the visiting room early if it got too crowded. The guards would let them rock out and they would end up having eight hour visits sometimes.

Everything was good for a while. The only problem was Bonnie was so consumed with being there for Karl, she never took the time to recognize she was still hurting because of all his past mistakes. The wounds were still there and she never took the time to heal properly.

"Of course I want to but how are we going to get the marriage license? I called the Chapel and they said there is no way to get it through the prison system."

"Well you can just handle that out there right?" he asked, anxiously.

"You have to be there though. We both have to go to city hall with our ID and social security cards and apply in person."

"Tell my brother Larry to go with you. You know that nigga look just like me."

"Baby he is nowhere near 6'2. They not gon' go for that."

"Just trust me, it'll work. They just want that bread anyway. You got my driver's license and Social security card. So, handle that alright?"

"I will. I love you baby," she said. "Talk to you in the morning."

"Alright baby. Love you too."

Karl was right when he said they would get away with it.

A nervous Bonnie, walked into room 413 at City Hall with Karl's brother Larry to apply for the marriage license. They filled out the application, paid eighty dollars cash and showed the necessary documents. Three days later, Bonnie went back to pick up the marriage license. Karl didn't want to wait, so the following week they were married by one of the pastors at the prison. Bonnie was wearing white pants and a white blazer. Her hair was pulled back in a bun. She looked very beautiful. Karl was wearing his burgundy jumpsuit and a pair of white ked sneakers, he hated so much. He told her as soon as he got home, he would buy her a huge rock and re-marry her. She didn't care she wasn't able to walk down the aisle in a beautiful wedding dress or that she wasn't able to exchange vows in front of all their family and friends. The union between them was all that mattered to her. They stood before one another, with bright smiles on their faces and exchanged the words "I DO."

Bonnie told everyone she married Karl. Most of them thought she was just plain ol' foolish to marry him while he was in jail. But none of them told her to her face. She kept her father in the dark about everything because she knew he wouldn't be happy about it. He didn't even know he was locked up at this point and Bonnie would keep it that way. She didn't want to hear any I told you so's.

One night, Monique invited Bonnie and Tess over to her house for girl's night. They ate and drank wine, while they watched their favorite movie "Waiting to Exhale." Somehow they got on the topic of their childhood's and Bonnie started talking about how it was with her mother. She told them stories about how Karen was good for breaking up homes and taking men for everything they had. Tess said, "Dag girl, you can write a book about that shit! Your mom was something else!" And at that very moment, a light bulb went off inside her head. *That's exactly what I'm gon' do. I'm gon' write a book about it.* She always had a gift for writing, ever since she was a little girl she would write poetry, short stories and screenplays but she never thought about actually writing a book.

Bonnie was at the point where she didn't want to work for anyone. She wanted to get money but be a boss at the same time, so she went into full hustle mode. A lot of different photographers reached out to Bonnie on social networking sites to do photo shoots, but she never followed up with any of them. Now she was thinking that getting into the urban modeling world wouldn't be such a bad idea. She figured, she would use modeling as a platform to build a name for herself, and then branch out and do other things.

"I like the book idea but I don't know about that modeling shit." Karl's face twisted, in annoyance.

"Why not? I'm smart. I know what I'm doing and I'm only gon' do it to see what kind of doors it can open up," she said, trying her hardest to get him onboard. "This is for the both of us. I don't want you to come home and start selling drugs again, only to go right back to jail. We have to start thinking about our future."

"You're right we do. But that doesn't mean I want you out there taking off your clothes and showing your body to mufuckas. Especially not my wife yo."

"Let me just do it for a little while and see how things go. Me coming to you first should make you feel secure in all of this. It's about us. I'm just tryna make sure we good."

"Alright Bonnie. Just don't let that modeling shit come between us and remember that we have a plan. Don't get caught up in that shit!" he said sharply.

"I won't baby. I won't…," she said. "What we have is solid. Nothing can come between us."

A few weeks later, Bonnie shot with a well-known photographer in New York City. He had a lot of connections in the industry, since he shot for most of the top urban magazines and was the go-to guy for all the video vixens and eye candy models. He'd been reaching out to Bonnie for months, dying to get her in front of his lens. She shot three different eye candy looks and she killed every single set. When the photographer released the images everyone wanted to know who this new Bonnie Summers chick was.

Meanwhile Bonnie started working on her book. Once she finished the introduction it was on and poppin' from there. Since she was writing about such a personal experience the process was smooth sailing for her. She would read parts of her book to Karl over the phone and he would say, "Damn B! You need to hurry up and finish that jawn!" All Karl did was read books in jail, so hearing his positive feedback gave her all the confidence she needed.

And though, Karl was the one in prison, Bonnie felt as though she was doing time with him. Most girls her age would've been out partying all hours of the night and getting at different players. Hell, it's not like Karl would have expected anything. He was only allowed to call twice a day, and the phones were turned off every night at 9 o'clock. So technically it would've been easy to do her and keep him satisfied at the same time. Crazy thing is that nothing felt the same without him. She didn't care to go out to clubs and she damn sure wasn't looking for anyone to replace him. Truth be told, even with him being incarcerated, she still believed no other man could fill his shoes. She spent many nights in bed, curled up like a baby and soaking her pillow with tears. There were also those times when she felt extremely lonely, and wished she had someone to hold her at night. But she would snap out of it and remind herself he didn't have life in prison and he would be coming home to her soon.

Jay reached out numerous times, when Karl was first sent to Mahanoy. A whole year went by, before she started getting with him. They would talk on the phone a lot and occasionally do lunch. He'd always liked Bonnie and wanted her for himself. Jay knew the hold Karl had on her was strong, so he settled for whatever he could get. And that was a platonic relationship. Still, she could never tell Karl she had anything to do with him. She knew he would lose it.

Bonnie started networking and shooting with other photographers in the industry. She met a makeup artist while on the set of a shoot and he gave her the contact info for

Slick Magazine. Slick Magazine was one of the top men's magazines on the shelves, and only the hottest vixens and celebrities graced the pages.

Bonnie submitted a few photos to the editor of the magazine and she received an email back from them the very next day. They told her to come into their office in Manhattan, so they could see her in person. She was told to bring a bikini, a pair of heels and to be prepared for a test shoot.

A week after Bonnie's test shoot, she received a call from the editor of the magazine asking her if she could be in Manhattan for a shoot. They planned on using Bonnie for a later shoot, but one of the girls cancelled and she was the first replacement that came to mind. She said yes and then rushed to get herself together last minute. First she went to the nail salon for a quick manicure and pedicure, and then hauled ass off to New York City.

When Bonnie arrived on set she felt like a star for real. They were shooting in a huge studio with beautiful sceneries set up for the girls. Everyone was so accommodating to her. The editor of the magazine greeted her with a hug and introduced her to the hairstylist and makeup artist. A flamboyant gay assistant rushed over to Bonnie, while she was getting her hair and makeup done, "Can I get you some water or something. Are you hungry? We ordered a variety of food," he said, with one hand on his hip. "Umm I'll have some water. Thank you," she replied. *Shit, I could sure get used to this kind of treatment!* she thought to herself.

"Gorgeous! I love it!" The photographer shouted out. "Now turn around and let me see that beautiful backside." Bonnie turned towards the camera and then arched her back, so her ass poked out even more. She put one finger in her mouth, and gave an enticing "Come and get it" look. "That's it! That's the shot!" he said, ecstatically. There were a dozen of people on set watching, as Bonnie posed for the camera half naked. She did a phenomenal job on her shoot and was told by the photographer that out of all five models he shot that day, she was the only one who brought her A game.

On the ride home Bonnie was smiling from the inside out. She couldn't believe she just finished shooting with Slick Magazine. There were girls who been in the modeling game for years and were still waiting on a callback from Slick Magazine. She was just happy everything was going as planned.

Bonnie made it home that night around seven o'clock. She took a hot shower, changed into her night clothes, climbed into bed and waited for Karl to call at their set time. The clock turned to eight thirty and Bonnie's phone rang. He was never a minute late.

"Hey baby," she answered, smiling.

"What's up. How'd your shoot go?"

"It went very well. They gon' feature me in the next issue."

"That's wassup B, I'm happy for you," he said. "You know they gon' be asking you all type of sex questions and shit for your interview."

"I know. I'm nervous about it too. I've never done an interview before."

"Don't even sweat it. When they ask you about your plans and what you got lined up, make sure that you talk about your book. That's free promotion, you feel me?"

"Yeah you're right," she said, admiring his hustler mentality.

"I gotchu tho baby, we gon' go over all that when you come up here next week."

"Okay baby. I love you. Can't wait to see you next week."

"I love you too and make sure you send me that freaky letter and those pictures."

"I gotchu," she said. "I'll have Monique take some pictures of me tomorrow."

"Dem last jawns you sent me, got damn! They had me bussin' all crazy." He laughed.

"Alright silly. I gotchu baby."

"Okay. Talk to you in the morning."

"Good night Karl."

When one of the editors called Bonnie for her interview, she was well prepared. She knew how to handle the sexual questions, and she also talked about her book she would be releasing and how she wanted her own publishing company someday. The issue was released in May and it was clear that Bonnie made quite an impression on them. She was featured on the contents page, and then her eight page spread followed. Her shots were very risqué but she looked absolutely stunning. Karl had actually seen it before she had. A lot of the inmates were subscribers and they would always get the new issues the day before they hit newsstands.

Karl felt like the man, because everyone on the block was giving him props for having such a bad wife. She represented for him too when she mentioned her dude was locked up, but she was going to hold him down until he got home. Karl's name stamped on her ass for all to see, made him feel like he was on top of the world. For the first time in a long time, everything was going great for the both of them.

CHAPTER TEN
You Used To Love Me

Now, it was two full years that Karl had been in prison and the weekly two and a half hour drive began taking a toll on Bonnie's vehicle. She'd never missed a visit, until one morning her car shut off when she pulled off the block. She cranked the ignition again and drove for about a mile and then it shut off again. She didn't want to risk being stranded way out in the middle of nowhere, so she went back home. It wasn't like Bonnie to be late for their visits, so when ten o'clock rolled around and his name wasn't called, Karl grew worried.

"What's up. You cool?"

"Yeah I'm alright. Something's wrong with the car though," she said. "It keeps cutting off and I didn't want to chance driving up there."

"Is that the first time it ever did that?"

"Yeah. You think it needs a tune-up or something?"

"Probably. You still got Ted's number right?"

"No. I never saved it in my phone."

"It's 267-259-1502. Call him and ask him to get it

checked out."

"Okay baby. I'll call him as soon as we hang up."

Even though Ted wasn't his right hand man or anything, he was one of the few friends he had left since most of them turned on him when he was arrested. Plus, Ted was the only one he could really trust around Bonnie. It took a lot for him to turn to another man and ask him to look after his woman, while he was away. He needed to make sure she was cool until he got home and he needed someone on the outside that could look out for her.

The next day, Ted told Bonnie to come down South Philly so he could have her car checked out. She didn't feel comfortable getting on the expressway though. She was afraid it would cut off again, so he came to her apartment and drove her car, while she followed him in his BMW.

The mechanic put the car on a diagnostic machine and found there was a bad sensor, which was causing the car to turn off. Since he would have to order the part and wait for it to be delivered, he told Ted to leave the car and it would be ready by the end of the week.

He didn't want Bonnie to be without transportation, so he drove her to one of his car lots and gave her a 2007 Lexus Coupe to drive until her car was ready. Out of all the cars Ted had, why would he give her something so luxurious to run around in just for a couple of days? What was he trying to prove? And why did he want to impress her?

"Ted, I'm on 19th and Mifflin. How do I get back to 76?" she asked.

"Bang a right on 18th, take 18th to Snyder and make a right. Make a left at the 25th street Bridge and it'll run you right into the expressway."

"Alright thanks. And thank you for helping me out with the car situation. We really appreciate it."

"No Problem," he said. "I'm gon' be your boyfriend until he comes home."

"C'mon that ain't cool," she said, in a disappointed voice. "That's supposed to be your man."

"I'm just playing with you Bonnie," he said, but Bonnie knew that he'd meant what he said. He was trying to feel her out to see if she would be down. "I'll let you know when your car is ready. In the meantime, let me know if you need anything."

"Okay Ted. Thanks."

On her ride home she thought about what Ted said to her and whether or not she should mention it to Karl. The last thing she wanted to do was upset him, especially while he was in jail. She knew if he was home, Ted would've never fixed his lips to say such a thing. She shut him down anyway and she felt there was no need to bring it up to Karl. Being locked up and away from the people you love was stressful enough. However, she did tell his mother and she too felt it was best not to mention it to Karl.

Over the next few weeks, Bonnie continued to go to work and on Thursdays she would go visit Karl. He was moved from a level three to a level two, which was a really good thing in prison. He was now in a work program and being recognized for his good behavior. They moved him on D block, where all of the inmates stayed out of trouble and were coming home soon. Karl tried his hardest to stay out the way and out of trouble so he could finish up his last three years and come home.

Memorial Day weekend was approaching, and it seemed as though the entire city of Philadelphia was going to Miami to celebrate. Monique and Tess were going and they were sick to death of Bonnie not enjoying herself. They weren't going to take no for an answer this time.

"Bonnie you're only twenty-two years old. Stop being a fucking grand mom," Monique teased.

"I'm not being a grand mom. I just don't feel like being bothered with that mess."

"Hell, your ass don't never feel like being bothered. When is the last time you've gone out? I know you love Karl and all but damn girl you still gotta live your life."

"She's right B. You can't just keep putting your life on

hold," Tess chimed in. "You're coming with us to Miami!"

"Karl is going to have a fit ya'll. I'm not going," she said.

"See that's the shit we talkin' bout. Stop letting that nigga control your every move."

"Alright ya'll, I'll go," she laughed. "Calm ya'll asses down."

When Bonnie told Karl that she was going to Miami he was livid. He said going out there wouldn't be appropriate being as though they were now married. But Bonnie knew even if they weren't married, he still wouldn't want her going. She told him she was going and tried to assure him she would be on her best behavior. He cursed her out something terrible and then hung up on her.

The following weekend, she and the girls flew out to Miami, Florida. They had a ball and it was exactly what Bonnie needed. Their hotel was right on the beach at Ball Harbour, on Collins Ave. Monique booked the hotel online and had no idea that it would be so far away from the action, but it worked out perfectly. The hotel was directly across the street from Miami's finest and upscale mall. When it was time to party they just caught a cab to South Beach, to whichever club was jumping.

The entire time that Bonnie was in Miami she didn't receive a single call from Karl, until Monday night when she got back to Philly. When she saw the 570 number appear on the caller id she just shook her head at his pettiness *Now this nigga wanna call.*

"What's up?" he said, in a nonchalant tone.

"Did you lose your damn mind?" she said. "You ain't call me in four whole days."

"I was giving you space. You said you wanted to start enjoying yourself right?" he asked, sarcastically.

"Here we go again with this shit," she said, while smacking her lips.

"Yeah I know. You getting tired of dealing with this jail shit right."

"What are you talking about? Where is this coming

from?"

"I'm talkin' about how different you been acting lately. You don't even write me as much as you used to. And the fact that you went to Miami when I told you not to, shows me you ain't feeling me like you used to."

"Are you fucking serious? I've been there to see you every week for two years straight. I've been there for you, riding for you, and I've been faithful!" she said, raising her voice. "What you mean I ain't feeling you like I used to?"

"You just ain't. Just like with that modeling shit. I told you I ain't want you doing that but you did it anyway."

"Wow. Just because I went to Miami, now you're finding a problem with everything. You said you were happy about the magazine feature. Hell, you even coached me on what to say in my interview."

"I only did that shit because you made it clear you were going to do it regardless of what I told you. I was only tryna support you. But I can't stand that shit. All of it," he said. "I don't respect that smut ass shit."

"You know what Karl, fuck you! You got a lot of nerves coming at me like this when all I ever did was try and be there for you! When I should've left your cheating ass a long fucking time ago! I should've left you when I caught you fucking that bitch in our bed, and I should've left you when I found out about you and that bitch Michelle! Fuck you!" she yelled through the phone and then hung up in his ear.

To Bonnie's surprise, Karl didn't call her back that night. He'd been feeling very insecure lately and his biggest fear was that Bonnie would start treating him like a jail nigga. He knew she was starting to move around and the last thing he wanted was for her to find someone else, which is why he tried to keep her on such a short leash. He still tried to control her moves, even from jail.

That night, Bonnie was so upset she called Jay's phone repeatedly. His voicemail kept picking up on the first ring. She sent him a text message *hit me ASAP I need to see you*. Still there was no response from him. Bonnie so desperately needed to be held, kissed and taken out of the negative state that she was in. Without a doubt, she'd planned on sleeping with him that night.

She thought it was strange when she didn't hear back from him but then two days later he called her from jail. He was at Monroe county jail, way up near the Poconos. He gave Bonnie the address and told her to write and send him pictures. He said he would be transferred to another prison in a few weeks, but he was unsure of where he'd be sent.

The next week, she wrote Jay and sent him a couple of pictures. They weren't the kind of pictures she sent Karl, just some regular flicks of her hanging out on the club scene. After four whole days Karl finally called Bonnie's phone, but this time he called her collect which was unusual. He always kept time on the phone and would only use the collect if he ran out, and wasn't able to make it to the commissary. When Bonnie heard the recording, *you have a collect call* instead of the usual, *you have a prepaid call*...she knew Karl had been reaching out to old friends.

"Yo. What's up?"

"What's up Karl," she replied, in a monotone voice.

"Listen Bonnie, the reason why I haven't called you is because I felt like I needed to give you some space. I don't want us to let this jail shit tear us apart," he said.

"You being in jail isn't tearing us apart. You're tearing us apart," she said. "My love for you hasn't changed."

"It's hard being in here away from you and sometimes my mind starts to wonder. It's not that I'm trying to control your life Bonnie. I know you're young and you have to live your life. I just don't want to lose you to another nigga."

"You don't have to worry about that. I'm not going nowhere. I'm gon' be right here to pick you up and take you away from here. We got two years in; lets get through these last three. We gon' be fine baby. I gotchu!" she said, trying to ease his fears.

"Thank you for saying that Bonnie. I love you."

"I love you too."

"There is something I want to talk to you about," he said. "I know what I want to do with my life when I get outta here."

"And what's that?"

"I'm gon' write books," he said. "You writing "Shadow of a Gold Digger" inspired me to write a book about my life and growing up in the streets."

"I think that's a great idea!" she said, ecstatically. "Baby we can start our own publishing company!"

"Yup K&B publishing," he said, smiling through the phone.

"Sounds good to me," she said.

Although she was happy to hear that his spirits were up and that he was back to thinking positive, she still believed he'd been up to something. She knew Karl inside and out, and she could feel that he'd been in contact with someone.

Over the next few weeks, Bonnie continued to go to work every day, except for on Thursdays when she would visit Karl. She focused real hard on completing her book, grinding hard, and keeping Karl sane. She knew what she had in Karl. Since day one she told him she felt as though he was better than just being a drug dealer. She always believed Karl could be something great and now he was finally starting to believe it himself.

One day, while at work Bonnie saw the number 570-773-2158 pop up on her caller id. Karl didn't usually call her while she was working. They had set times but she thought maybe he missed her and wanted to hear her voice. But to her surprise it was Jay. Out of all the jails he could've been transferred to, he was sent to the same prison as Karl.

She wasn't going to risk Karl finding out she was in contact with him. She told herself she wouldn't have anything to do with him while he was at Mahanoy. No mail, no more accepting his phone calls and of course she wouldn't be visiting him.

Now that Bonnie knew how Karl really felt about her modeling, she began falling back from it. Plus, she started to see that there was no real money in the urban modeling game. On the flipside, she formed a lot of good relationships with people in the industry, and she planned on using all of her modeling connections to help promote her book.

The day before Bonnie's visit, she started having car trouble again. Her car kept running hot and it caused it to shut down. When Karl called her, she told him she wouldn't be able to make their visit. He said to call Ted so he could have the car fixed. Calling Ted was the last thing she wanted to do. She hated the fact she had to call him for help, especially since he'd come on to her.

"Naw I'm tired of turning to him for everything."

"We gotta do what we have to for right now."

"It's looking like we need him though," she said. "I'm not calling him."

"Fuck you mean! All you should be worried about is getting up here to see me!" he shouted.

"That's all you care about! Fuck me and everything else, as long as I can make it up there to see you every week. That's all that matters!" she spat back.

"How is that all I care about? I ran through damn near all my money in here tryna make sure you cool!"

"I'm so sick of this back and forth shit with you."

"Well then fuck it Bonnie. I know you wanna leave me anyway," he said. "Don't call him. You ain't gotta come up here to see me."

"Fine. I won't," she said.

"I'm tired of being stressed out in here," he said, in a pitiful voice. "I'm out," he said and then hung up the phone.

Hearing the sadness in Karl's voice made Bonnie feel terrible inside. She hated when they had these spats. It would literally mess up her mood and her entire day. Thursday came and not being able to visit him really put Bonnie in a bad place. She didn't want to call Ted but she didn't have a choice. She knew he would let her borrow a car and she desperately wanted to see Karl's face. She just wanted to kiss him, hold him in her arms and tell him everything was going to be okay.

Friday morning, she drove up to Mahanoy in a car that Ted gave her. The entire ride, something didn't feel right and when she pulled into the parking lot an uneasy feeling came over her. She walked into the building and to the front desk. She was greeted by Officer Green, who would always process her visit as soon as she walked through the door. Bonnie smiled at him and said, "Atkins HQ5277." He entered the information into the computer and then gave Bonnie a look as if something was wrong.

"He can't have any visits today," he said. "He went out yesterday."

"What? Who came to see him?" she asked, hoping and praying that it was a family member.

"You know I'm not supposed to give out that information," he said.

"C'mon, I won't say anything. Please tell me," she said, anxiously.

"It was Vicky Blunt." The name Vicky registered in Bonnie's brain instantly. Could this be the same Vicky that called Karl's phone years ago? The one who he told not to call him anymore because he had a girlfriend.

"Wow. Were they on a visit long?"

"Yup it looks like they were out there for six hours."

"Okay, thanks," she said, and then walked away. She rushed out to her car, with tears building up in her eyes. *Who and the hell does he think he is? This nigga wants to cheat on me from jail...no fuck this shit!* she said to herself. She wiped her tears and went back inside. She knew Jay put her on his visiting list when he was at the Monroe County Jail, and all of his information transferred over to Mahanoy. She walked back to the front desk and said, "I want to see Jayson Gibson."

"Uh oh. What are you doing Bonnie?" he said, with a smirk on his face.

"Nothing. He's my cousin. I drove all this way I'm gon' get a visit with somebody," she said.

"What's his PP#?"

"I don't have it. But his DOB is 06/11/1978."

"I found him," he said.

Bonnie sat in the waiting room anxiously waiting for her name to be called. She was furious with Karl and was ready to show him just how much. She was tired of being let down, and embarrassed by him. She put up with all his bullshit over the years and she refused to let him play her from jail.

When Bonnie got to the visiting room, she saw a lot of familiar faces and it seemed as though all eyes were on her. When Jay saw Bonnie's face, he couldn't believe what she'd just done. Right at that moment, he knew an entire beef was created between he and Karl.

The guard that supervised the visiting room didn't like what he saw. He walked over to Bonnie and told her to come with him. She followed him to the front desk, and he began scolding her as if she was his child.

"What are you doing out here with him?" he said. "How did you even get in?"

"That's my cousin. And what do you mean how did I get in?"

"You're not allowed to be on two inmate's visiting list at the same time."

"I didn't know that."

"The only way you can stay here is if you request to be taken off of Karl's visiting list," he said. "So is it going to be Jayson's or Karl's?

"Keep me on Karl's," she said, but not quite understanding why she chose to stay on his list. In her mind she was done with him.

"Okay. Well then I have to end your visit," he said, in a firm voice.

Bonnie walked over to Jay and told him she was being asked to leave. He stood there with an irked expression on his face but not because she had to leave. He was pissed that she dragged him into she and Karl's mess.

"I hope you know Karl is gon' find out about this," he said.

"So what," she said. "I don't care."

"I care. I'm tryna come home, not get more time for getting into some nut shit in here. You really put me in a bad situation."

"I didn't mean to. I'm sorry," she said, sincerely.

"Alright Bonnie," he said, before walking away. He didn't hug her or anything. The only thing that was on his mind was the confrontation that he knew was near.

Bonnie left out of the prison not feeling any regret whatsoever. In fact, she couldn't wait until Karl heard about what happened. It was about time that she'd given him a taste of his own medicine. At this point, all she wanted was sweet revenge.

It only took about a half hour before she received the phone call she'd been waiting for. The second Karl called she pulled over on the side of the road, so she could get at him the way she wanted to.

"Bitch did you lose your fucking mind?" he yelled through the phone.

"And pussy did you lose yours? You got me fucked up. You had that bitch Vicky up there yesterday!" she screamed. "Yeah I know all about it dickhead!"

"Yeah and so what! She helping me with my book."

"Oh really? This bitch is helping you with your book? Even more enough reason to be done with your ass. How fucking dare you! I gave you that idea and you pulling this ugly, boney bitch in to help you!"

"You went too far this time Bonnie. And I promise you when I get to the yard; I'm fucking that nigga up! He knows not to play with me like that!" he said, raising his voice.

"Do what you gotta do. I don't care anymore."

"You been stopped caring anyway. You used to love me Bonnie but I ain't no damn fool. I could feel when it all changed."

"Save all that bullshit. You know you fucked up," she said. "Don't try and flip it on me."

"I don't care what you say; you don't do me like that.

You got all these niggas in my business and shit."

"There you go worrying about the wrong thing. Listen to me when I tell you this…I'm gon' get you back and I'm gon' get you back good," she said. "I had enough of this. I'm done!"

CHAPTER ELEVEN
Long Way Down

"**I** used to think that I wasn't fine enough, and I used to think that I wasn't wild enough, but I won't waste my time tryna figure out why you playing games, what's this all about..." Keyshia Cole blasted through the speakers of Bonnie's car while she sang along, feeling every single word.

When she got back to Philly she called Ted to find out whether or not her car was ready. He told her it would be ready in a couple of days and she could keep his car until then. Right before he hung up the phone Bonnie blurted out, "You won't believe what just happened." She desperately needed to vent and besides, she wanted everyone to know what a piece of shit he was for cheating on her from jail.

"What?"

"I couldn't even get in cause Karl had another bitch up there already...some bitch named Vicky," she said. "He didn't know I was coming. I wanted to surprise him."

"Damn you been holding him down all this time. Why would he do some shit like that?"

"I asked myself the same thing. And I've come to the conclusion he ain't never gonna change. He's been cheating on me since day one. I'm done with him Ted. I don't want him anymore."

"You ain't done. You love that nigga," he said. "He loves you too. Shit he loves you to death. I don't know why he fucking up."

"I don't even care to know why. I'm off him."

"Between me and you, I always thought you were too good of a girl to be with him. We all did, when he used to hit on you and shit, me and my homeys would be like damn, she doesn't deserve that."

"I know. I guess love is blind sometimes," she said, in a sad tone.

"C'mon let me take out to eat," he said. "I'ma try to take your mind off of everything."

"Hmm…I don't know," she said, but then something went off inside of her, when she thought about Karl and his disregard for her feelings. *Fuck it*, she thought. "Okay. I'll go."

"You wanna come meet me down here or you want me to come get you?"

"Come get me from my house," she said. "What time are we getting together?"

"I'll be there to get you at six."

"Alright cool. Call me when you on your way."

"Alright."

When Bonnie hung up the phone she couldn't believe she just made plans to go out with Karl's homey. She knew it was very wrong, but still she wanted to go through with it. She was tired of being hurt and let down by him and although she was in denial about it, she saw Ted as her revenge.

He called Bonnie at six o'clock on the dot, and told her he was parked out front. She peeked out of the window and saw his BMW parked across the street. She looked at herself in the mirror to make sure her hair was still intact, and then she put on her six-inch thigh high Chanel boots, grabbed her pocket book and left out the door.

"Damn you look good," he said. "You smell good too."

"Thank you," she said, with a smile on her face. "You look good too."

"You ever eat at Del Frisco's?" he asked.

"No, I haven't. But I heard the food is really good."

"Alright cool. Let's shoot down there then," he said.

After dinner Ted asked Bonnie if she wanted to catch a movie but she suggested bowling instead. They drove way out to Doylestown, so they wouldn't run into anyone. While Ted was driving he couldn't stop glancing over at Bonnie. Since the first day Karl had introduced him to her, he thought she was the most beautiful girl he'd ever laid eyes on. And the day he told Bonnie he wanted to be her boyfriend until Karl came home, he wasn't joking one bit. But Ted had no idea just how deep things would get.

They had a good time that night. Bonnie didn't think about the crazy drama with Karl the entire time she was with him. What she liked most about him was, he was so different from Karl. He was quiet, and humble but thorough at the same time. He didn't sell drugs and had never been arrested in his life. What attracted Bonnie the most, was his boss status and Bonnie loved a boss player.

Ted called Bonnie every day that week and would say, "What we doing today?" Neither one of them knew exactly what they were getting themselves into. All they knew, was they liked spending time with one another. Even though this was something she wasn't proud of, she was still dying to tell someone. As much as she loved her girl Tess she didn't tell her because she knew she was going to tell her how wrong it was. And she was in no mood for that. She needed someone who would ride and co-sign her scandalous behavior, so of course she confided in Monique.

"Girl do you and stop tripping! It ain't like they best friends. They never even hung out did they?" Monique said.

"No, they only did business together. I mean don't get me wrong they got love for one another but they aren't that tight," she said. "Still, if he ever found out it would be some shit girl."

"Girl, Ted is not gonna let this shit get out…trust me! You know what I think about the whole situation! Do you, cause these niggas damn sure gon' do them," she said, all hype.

Bonnie laughed. "Girl you ain't never lied!" she said. "I'm not gon' worry myself about it…it is what it is."

For about a week straight Bonnie ignored all of Karl's phone calls. She wasn't feeling him at all in the first place and then he had the audacity to write a very nasty letter putting the entire blame on her for what happened.

Bonnie,

It's clear to me you forgot who the fuck I am. I can't even believe you would have enough heart to play with me like that. And just so you know you got ol' boy fucked up. I whooped his bitch ass! You crossed the line with this shit. It's over, I'm done. You've lost all respect for me Bonnie and it's all because I've been here too long. You treating me just like a jail nigga and I'd rather you just walk away from me now and go head before I really start hating you. I know I fucked up and did a lot of wrong. I treated you bad. I'm not denying any of it. But you won't let it go. You constantly throw that shit in my face and keep beating me with my past mistakes. Why did you wait almost three years to do this shit to me? You should've been left! You should've been told me you didn't want to do this bid with me. I would've understood because of everything I did to you Bonnie. But this right here is the worst thing you could do to me. That's the only reason why I let the bitch Vicky come up here and see me. I just needed someone to remind me of who I am. I got tired of being looked at as weak by you. I'm moving on though Bonnie. And I'm sure you already have. Why would you be faithful to a nigga that did you so wrong? Why would you wait for me, when all you do is talk about how I hurt you? Fuck outta here! I know you fucking and all that! But it's cool keep doing you! Live your life B! I'm out!

After reading Karl's letter she was furious. And she knew this part oh so well. Whenever Karl would get caught doing wrong he would try and flip the script, by putting the blame on her. Bonnie loved Karl more than anything in the world and in her heart she believed she would be the one to pick him up from jail and take him home. Once on a visit, she told him she was going to be standing next to a limousine, wearing a fur coat, waiting for him to walk out those prison doors, just like the chick Karen from the movie Goodfellas. He loved it when Bonnie talked like that. It would make him all warm inside and literally melt his heart. Karl was wrong in thinking her love for him had changed. The real problem was, she still held on to the past and was very resentful towards him. There was a very thin line between the love and hate she felt for him. And his cheating from jail only made matters worse. It made her feel like he would come home and go right back to his old ways.

Bonnie finally answered Karl's phone call, and to her surprise he spoke to her in a very humble tone. He apologized to her and expressed how badly he needed to see her. Although she made a promise to herself she would never step foot inside that prison again…she broke that promise and went to visit him the following day.

Once in Karl's arms, she felt a rush of emotions. There was no denying she still loved him. But when she looked in his eyes she saw someone who she couldn't trust with her heart. She thought to herself *would he try so hard to hold on to me if he were home? And what if I wait for him and he comes home only to do me the same way he did before?* And the fact he was already in contact with women from his past, didn't sit well with Bonnie.

Even though she smiled and talked to him for hours as If everything was okay, she made a conscious decision she wasn't going to wait for him. She didn't want to do him dirty though. She still planned on being there for Karl but she knew it was only a matter of time before he slipped up again.

A few months passed, and Bonnie was still juggling both Karl and Ted. She managed to complete her first novel "Shadow of a Gold Digger" and she was thrilled about it. Karl suggested that Bonnie send it to him so he could pass it around and get feedback from some of the other inmates.

Karl read the entire book in one day and he passed it on to some of his homies on the block, that were really into reading books. They all had nothing but positive things to say about Bonnie's book. Karl told Bonnie, "You need to go head and submit that jawn to a few publishers! You got some heat on your hands!"

Bonnie's relationship with Ted took an unexpected turn. She knew Ted was the playboy type and he had lots of women. She wasn't looking for anything serious with him. She just enjoyed spending time with him, and with Karl being away he filled a void in her life. As time went on, their feelings for one another grew stronger. She began seeing him for who he truly was. He was a good man, a good father and he was just good to people in general. He didn't have enemies; no one spoke negatively about him. If you asked anyone in the streets if they knew him they would say, "Oh yeah! That's my man…real good dude!" After spending years with Karl and his rugged lifestyle, this was quite refreshing to Bonnie.

One night, Ted took Bonnie over to Atlantic City to see Maxwell live in concert. After the show, they ate at a fancy restaurant and then went to the Tropicana. They messed around at the craps table all night, and Bonnie blew all of the money he'd given her on the slot machines. Ted already booked a luxurious suite for them there, so they wouldn't have to drive back in the wee hours of the morning. Plus, he thought it would be the perfect scenery for he and Bonnie to finally get intimate. She'd been holding out for months and he was dying to know what it felt like to be inside her.

Bonnie held out for two main reasons…she didn't want him to think she was a smut and she didn't want to be played out by him. In the back of her mind, she was worried he was just curious to know what it felt like to fuck Karl's girl, the one who he bragged about and loved so much. Karl always spoke highly of Bonnie and would tell anyone in a heartbeat he had the baddest bitch in the city. She feared he'd run his mouth and tell all of his friends he slept with her. The last thing she wanted was to be played out like that.

Enough time passed and she was over all the nonsense. Now she knew he developed real and deep feelings for her. The moment they walked into their hotel suite, they both knew what was about to go down. Bonnie hadn't had sex in three years and her pussy was throbbing for some action.

He anxiously undressed Bonnie from the waist down, laid her on the bed and then began giving her oral pleasure. She moaned as he made little circles around her clit and worked her inside. She gripped the sheets and the more he licked, the more intense she panted. "Take your clothes off; I need you to fuck me right now!" she said, after climaxing. He climbed on top of Bonnie and entered her wet and inviting vagina, "Damn this pussy wet. And it's tight as shit," he said. He became more excited, and he began thrusting his hard penis deeper inside of her...so deep that she could feel the tip of his dick tapping her cervix. "Yeah you my bitch now, you hear me? This my pussy now," he called out as he pumped faster and harder. They made wild and passionate love all night long and Bonnie loved every minute of it.

And from that day forward, they were officially a couple. Ted told Bonnie to move in with him, but she wasn't down to live in anybody's South Philly neighborhood. So, Ted told Bonnie to find a house in the suburbs. In the meantime, he moved his clothes into Bonnie's apartment. Everything happened so fast. One minute they were creeping and the next minute they were full blown boyfriend and girlfriend.

There was no more keeping it on the hush hush. Ted told all of his homies about him and Bonnie. A mutual friend of he and Karl said, "She a good girl man. He ain't treat her right anyway. Now you got her and he gotta swallow that shit, cause it's all part of the game." Funny thing was, there wasn't one person against it. Bonnie knew a few of Ted's friends through Karl, and none of them treated her any different when she came around with Ted.

But now everything was out in the open and Bonnie knew word would eventually hit the prison blocks. Hell, half of the time people locked up knew the 411 before the streets did. She was still seeing Karl every week and talking to him daily. She found herself in a crazy predicament, because here she was living with his friend and Ted was under the impression she and Karl were over.

As time went on, the visits became less and she wasn't writing him as much as she used to. Karl began to lean on Vicky more and more for support. Vicky wanted to be the woman in Karl's life for such a long time, but it was something about her that just didn't do it for him. For starters, she wasn't attractive enough. She was 5'11, skinny, bland and had zero sex appeal. There were times when Karl would be on a visit with Vicky, and he would get pissed that it was her instead of Bonnie, sitting next to him. It didn't help that Vicky would constantly bring Bonnie's name up, "What's going on with you and Bonnie?" Karl would instantly become irate and shut her down, "Why you always worried about her? I don't wanna fucking talk about her!"

Karl stressed many nights thinking about Bonnie and wondering who she'd been seeing. Who was taking her from him? He knew someone else had Bonnie's attention but never in a million years did he ever think it would be someone so close to home.

Dear Karl,

First off I want to say that I love you more than you'll ever know. I know I haven't been up there to see you and I haven't been writing you as much. Truth is, I'm really confused right now about a lot of things when it comes to us. It kills me that we're in this awkward place with one another but at the same time I feel as though space is necessary. I'm still not over a lot of the things you put me through and I hate feeling like whenever we have an argument you turn to other women. I feel like I have to walk on egg shells with you in order to keep you faithful and that shit ain't cool. You've taken me for granted over the years and you continue to do so. How do I know you won't come home and go back to your old ways? You say you've changed and all you want and need is me…then why are you still communicating with other bitches? You had an excuse for dealing with Michelle. You said you were afraid I would leave you, now three years later, what's your excuse for this Vicky bitch? Time after time you show me you don't take this marriage seriously. I can't trust you Karl and because of that I need time away from you to be on my own. I'm dropping your car off to your mom's house. That way you can sell it if you need to and put the money up. I still love you. That will never change.

Your Wife,
Bonnie

After reading Bonnie's letter he rushed out of his cell and onto the floor. He signed up for phone time at 8:30, but he was so desperate to speak to her, he found an inmate to switch times with. He nervously dialed Bonnie's number. He was afraid she wouldn't answer and even more afraid of what she would say if she did.

"Hey Bonnie," he said, in a mellow tone. "I just got your letter."

"You did?"

"Yeah, and I'm fucked up right now," he said. "Why don't you just be honest with me? You found somebody else right?"

"No. I haven't. Karl I just need some time to myself."

"That's bullshit. How and the fuck you need time to yourself when I'm locked up?" he said, raising his voice. "You said this shit before about taking a break. What the fuck sense does that make?"

"It doesn't have to make sense to you but it makes perfect sense to me. I need a break from all this shit. You, your lies, your cheating and all this fucking stress. Point, blank, period!"

"I told somebody what you said about time apart and the first thing they said was, you were seeing someone else."

"Oh boy, here we go. Which one of your bitches did you go running to? Was it that alien looking bitch Vicky?" she spat. "You always run to other bitches!"

"You fucking right! It was Vicky and she been here the whole time you been treating me like shit! She been keeping me from falling apart!"

"Wow. Are you fucking serious? I been riding with your cheating ass for three years and you got the fucking audacity to say, she been keeping you from falling apart?" Bonnie felt a rage come over her. He pushed her way over the edge with that remark. "You're so disrespectful, I fucking hate you! That's exactly why I don't want you anymore!"

"I hate you too bitch! You think I'm gon' kiss your ass and beg you to stay here with me, you wanna leave? Fuck it, leave then!" he said, out of anger.

"Well fuck you then! I am seeing somebody. And he's nothing like you. He's a good man and he's good to me. As a matter of fact, you know who he is," she said. "You know him very well."

"Fuck you mean I know who he is?" Karl said, trying to put the pieces together.

"Yup you sure do. And I want to thank you for introducing me to him. Good looking out," she said, spitefully.

"Yo Bonnie I hope you not talkin' about who I think you talkin' about," he said, in a low voice. "T?"

"Yup," she said, but then instantly regretted it once the words left her mouth. She couldn't believe she just admitted to fooling around with one of his homeys.

"Damn Bonnie is this you getting me back?" he asked. "Don't do me like this B."

"It's not about getting you back Karl. It's just something that happened."

"Bonnie do you hear what you telling me?" She remained silent on the other end of the phone. "You telling me that you fucking with my man. The nigga I told to look out for you and make sure you was cool."

"You pushed me to him," she said.

"I pushed you to fuck my homey? I'm bout to call this bitch ass nigga right now!" he said, hatefully.

Karl hung the phone up in Bonnie's ear and immediately dialed Ted's number. *No wonder why this pussy ain't been answering my calls…he been fucking my bitch*, Karl thought to himself. Karl got Ted's voicemail, so he hung up and tried again. This time Ted answered on the first ring. Karl stood there anxiously listening to the recording, waiting to be connected.

"It could've been anybody but not her. Not her T," Karl said.

"What you talkin' bout?" he asked.

"Nigga you know what I'm talkin' bout. Don't play me," he said. "I'm talkin' bout you and Bonnie."

"Naw man, where you hear that shit from?"

"And yo bitch ass gon' lie about the shit. You ain't even man enough to tell me the truth. Bonnie already told me. Nigga don't you know I will kill for her. That's mine right there. You don't touch mine," he said.

And although Ted was in the wrong, Karl talking to him in such a derogatory manner, only made him furious. They began going back and forth shooting nasty words at one another, until Karl had enough of the screaming match. "Pussy just remember I don't have life and when I get home it's on!" And Ted responded, "Well fuck it then, it's on."

Karl hung up the phone feeling worse than ever. He walked back on the block with his head hung low, trying to fight the tears. He knew it was over between him and Bonnie and the thought of her being with Ted was unbearable. He sat on the edge of his bunk; put his hands on his head and tears began rolling down his face. The pain he felt was real. He was truly broken up inside. Karl thought about all the times he'd done Bonnie wrong, and especially the times when he mistreated her in front of his friends. Everything was hitting him all at once, and he felt as though his world was falling apart.

That night was the toughest night to get through. The continuous thoughts of Bonnie lying next to Ted drove him crazy and kept him up all night. He envisioned them doing all of the things he used to do with Bonnie. Karl listened to WDAS every night and on this night it seemed as though every song that came on reminded him of Bonnie. When,

Atlantic Starr's "Send for me" came on he broke down even more. "Goodbye doesn't mean a thing with you and I, our love has stood through all the tests of time, if you're planning to leave me behind, let me put one more thing on your mind. If you ever need me baby, send for me…" The words resonated with Karl on so many different levels. Inside, he felt like someone had just torn his heart apart.

He made one last attempt to reach out to Bonnie, and in his very last letter he poured his heart out…

Bonnie,

I'm sitting here fucked up and in disbelief of what has happened to us. I guess all my past mistakes have finally caught up with me. I question if you really care about how serious that situation is with dude. I say that to say this; it's so serious that one of us might die over this shit. That's how bad I feel crossed by this mutherfucka. It's just that personal! He's a bitch and he doesn't play with guns, but he may try to pay somebody to holler at me because he's gonna be that scared when I come home. How the fuck did I get myself in this situation? How the fuck did you let this happen to us Bonnie? We've taken a turn for the worse. I always felt in my heart that I was coming home to you. Now, it's clear that it's not going to happen like that. At times, I feel like fuck it. I blame myself for my errors, but I also blame him for this shit. A real nigga would've never crossed his man. So now I have nothing. I don't have you, coming home to nothing and that's just fucked up. I can't lie Bonnie, this shit hurts deep, but you can't feel me or know how crushed I am by this. Your thing is, "you wouldn't feel like this if you were home." Bonnie this would've never happened if I were home and you know that. I thought we overcame a lot of hurdles and became a team but as you say you've changed. Now you're different. So different that mutherfuckas can come between us. But they have no idea they're coming in between something that I've always wanted. The person I love more than anything. Fucking my life up more than it already is. Inside of me is a hurricane that's worse than Katrina. The only way I can curb this anger is revenge…and Bonnie I will get it. I promise you that. That pussy is gonna feel my wrath.

Karl's letter left Bonnie feeling like shit. All the anger she felt towards him disappeared and all she wanted to do was hold him in her arms… but it was too late to turn back now. Everything was out in the open and she knew Karl would never look at her the same. Crazy thing is, she still loved him the same. And Bonnie had no idea what she'd just done. Maybe it was all the built up hurt, and frustration. Her thinking he would come home only to treat her dirty, or the fact he was still seeing Vicky. Whatever it was that pushed Bonnie to the point of no return…it destroyed their love forever.

CHAPTER TWELVE
Thanks For My Child

Three months later, Ted and Bonnie were in their new home. Bonnie found a beautiful town home in Huntington Valley. It was a beautiful quiet residential neighborhood. A couple of players from the Sixers and the Philadelphia Eagles resided in their community. Bonnie opened Ted up to a whole new world. He was a city boy, born and raised in South Philly. Even after all the money he made, he never left. Bonnie schooled him and showed him that when you getting money, you can't surround yourself with bums. She told him, "A boss should never be so accessible. Niggas should never know where you lay your head."

Bonnie didn't hear from Karl in months. In fact, he had no way of getting in contact with her. Ted made her change her cell number so he couldn't reach her anymore. She also filed for divorce and served Karl his papers in jail. She did all of this to prove to Ted she was seriously letting Karl go, but in the back of his mind there would always be doubt.

Karl leaned on Vicky for support and she played her part in being there for him. She didn't care she was a rebound chick. She was just happy to be in Bonnie's position. Karl still yearned for Bonnie's love and affection but Vicky definitely helped him cope through the most difficult time of his life. He was almost finished with his bid, and he was anxiously anticipating his return. He only had two more years to go. He had a serious Vendetta with Ted, and a whole lot to prove to Bonnie. He couldn't wait to go home, get back on his feet and shit on the ones that turned on him.

One morning, Bonnie awoke and was feeling extremely nauseous. She ran to the bathroom, holding her stomach and vomited into the toilet. She gargled some mouthwash, and wiped her face with a cold rag. She knew this feeling all too well, so she ran to the drug store to pick up a pregnancy test.

When Bonnie saw two lines appear on the urine stick she almost fainted. She took a picture of the positive pregnancy test and sent it to Ted's phone. She called Monique and then Monique called Tess on a three-way. By now, Tess knew that Bonnie and Ted were together and she actually liked him for Bonnie. The only thing she didn't approve of was them creeping. But now they were together and she loved them as a couple. She believed Ted brought a sense of stability and calmness into Bonnie's life.

"Oh my gosh, Bonnie!" Tess said, excitedly. "You're keeping it right?"

"I don't know girl. I want too but…," she said.

"But what?"

"Yeah girl, but what?" Monique butted in.

"If I have this baby, that means me and Karl are done forever. He'll never be able to get over that."

"Are you serious! You divorced that nigga and now you're with his friend. He's never gonna get over that. So you need to stop thinking that one day ya'll gon' be able to get back together," Monique said.

"She's right Bonnie. Why are you even with Ted if you still love Karl?" Tess asked.

"I don't know. I was just angry with Karl and somehow I let things get outta control," she said.

"Well Bonnie even if you get an abortion, and later on you get back with Karl, it will never work because he'll always throw Ted in your face," Tess said.

"Yeah you guys are right. Besides, Ted is a good man

and I know he'll be a great father," she said. "I'm just gon' forget all about me and Karl. I'm gon' have my baby."

"Good! I'm so happy for you Bonnie. You're gonna be a great mother!" Tess said.

"Yes you are! I'm so excited, I can't wait. We gotta start picking out names and everything!" Monique said, ecstatically.

Bonnie received a text message from Ted that read, *I wanted to get you pregnant. This made my day baby. I love you.* The way he responded to her being pregnant was confirmation she was making the right decision in keeping their child.

Two weeks later, Bonnie had become severely ill. She was so sick she couldn't even get out of bed. And whenever she did it was because she was running to the bathroom to vomit. Since, she wasn't able to keep anything down she was drastically losing weight. The doctors would tell her to eat peanuts, saltine crackers, and drink plenty of water. They even told her to suck on fresh lemons but nothing would cure this morning sickness. It got so bad that she went to the ER at Abington Memorial hospital and was admitted for dehydration. They hooked Bonnie up to an IV, so she could get nutrients.

The Doctor diagnosed Bonnie with Hyperemesis Gravidarum, a condition that causes severe nausea and vomiting, during pregnancy. The doctors prescribed Bonnie a medication called Phenergan and for the first two weeks it helped a great deal. Once she became immune to the drug she began experiencing the morning sickness all over again. This time the doctors prescribed Zofran, a drug that was given to cancer patients to prevent nausea caused by chemotherapy. Just like with the other drug, it only relieved her symptoms temporarily.

Ted was gone a lot during the day and although he saw how severely sick Bonnie was, he didn't make an effort to stay in and take care of her. Monique and Tess were both working full-time jobs but they stopped by as much as they could. Bonnie was glued to her bed and was absolutely miserable. Even though Bonnie wasn't ready to tell her father about being pregnant, she knew if he was aware of how ill she was, he would be there for her without a doubt.

Surprisingly, he didn't react to her pregnancy in the way she imagined he would. He first asked who the father was, and she had a long, drawn out conversation about how good of a guy Ted was and that he would really like him for her. Michael responded, "You're a smart girl and I know you wouldn't have a baby by a knucklehead. I do need to meet him however." He also told Bonnie he was looking forward to being a grandfather.

Michael always thought no one was good enough for his daughter but when he met Ted he actually liked him. He told Bonnie he seemed like a good dude and that they both complimented each other well. If he would've known she met him through Karl, Michael definitely would've sung a different tune.

He came over to Bonnie's house every afternoon to cook and clean for her, while she was coping with her severe morning sickness. By the time Bonnie turned sixteen weeks, the morning sickness ceased and she couldn't have been more thrilled about it. Now she didn't have to be confined to the bed all day. She was ready to get her life back.

Bonnie made sure she looked good pregnant. She wasn't one of those chicks who used pregnancy as an excuse to look ratchet. She still went to the gym every other day and she went out in her six- inch Giuseppe Zanotti heels, dressed to kill. Men still tried to holler at Bonnie, with her big belly and all. Everyone told her she had that pregnancy glow and being pregnant was very becoming.

At Bonnie's twenty week prenatal visit she found out she was having a boy. She called Ted right away to deliver the good news because all he talked about was having a lil' T. Bonnie on the other hand, wasn't so thrilled about having a boy. She just knew she was having a girl, and when people said they could tell she was going to have a boy because of the way she was carrying, she would argue them up and down.

Ted was still in disbelief Bonnie was really going to have his baby. A part of him believed she still loved Karl and she would go back to him when he was released. Bonnie going through with the pregnancy made him feel more secure in their relationship. Some nights he would look over at her lying next to him and he would think to himself, *Damn I can't believe I'm really with Karl's girl.*

Throughout Bonnie's entire pregnancy she and Ted still carried on as they did before she got pregnant. They went out to dinner twice a week, and spent one day on the weekend together at the movies, bowling, AC or sometimes they drove to NYC. Their sex life was still on and poppin' as well. They would get it in every night just as they did before.

One night while lying in bed, Bonnie turned to Ted and started kissing him all over. She proceeded to go down on him but he stopped her and said he was tired. It was the first time he'd ever told her no and she was confused as to why. She didn't push the issue however. She just rolled over and went to bed.

The next evening, they went to the movies, and on their way home Bonnie said to him, "I'm so horny right now; it's going down when we get home." He looked at her and said, "Remember that rash I had on my foot? I went to the hospital and the doctor told me I have an infection in my body." Bonnie just looked at him with a confused look on her face.

"What do you mean you have an infection in your body?" she asked.

"I don't know. That's what the doctor's told me," he said. "They gave me a shot in my butt and said it should be cleared up in a week.

"A shot?" she asked, with one eyebrow raised. "So what you got an STD?"

"Fuck no," he said.

"So why are we even having this conversation? I told you I was horny and now you're telling me about some infection in your body."

"I was just letting you know I wasn't trying to have sex until this infection clear up," he said, digging a deeper hole for himself.

"Seriously you need to let me know what's up. I'm seven months pregnant. If you got something then I need to know," she said, in a concerned voice.

"Baby relax. You cool. Stop worrying about nothing," he said.

But Bonnie knew better. Even Ray Charles could see something wasn't right. Bonnie followed her instinct and at her next prenatal visit she told the doctor to give her an STD check. Luckily she had because two days later she received a call back from her OBGYN stating she tested positive for Gonorrhea. Bonnie's heart dropped to the floor. Not only was she hurt he'd cheated on her, but he knew he had something and didn't even tell her. Knowing she was carrying his child, how could he put her and his unborn child's health at risk?

After hanging up with her doctor she immediately called Ted's phone. When he answered she didn't snap on him or even raise her voice. The moment she said her doctor called, Ted already knew what was coming next.

"She told me I have Gonorrhea. I was just tested for everything two months ago. So that means you just contracted it," she said. "Who you been fucking?"

"I'm sorry Bonnie but I swear to you, I didn't fuck anybody. All I did was get my dick sucked."

"I don't believe you Ted. I think you did more than that. What kills me the most is that you knew you had it and didn't tell me."

"I was afraid to tell you Bonnie. I'm sorry. It won't happen again."

"Yeah. Alright," she said, before hanging up in his ear.

Bonnie got off the phone feeling like shit. She started thinking about Karl and how he never brought home an STD. *Damn I guess the grass ain't always greener on the other side,* she thought to herself. She was disgusted with him, and the trust went right out the door. But what was she to do now? She left Karl, divorced him while in jail, moved on with his friend and was now seven months pregnant. Too far gone…to turn back now.

Bonnie was dying to get into Ted's voicemail, so she called her little private detective Monique. Monique was good for snooping and cracking boyfriend's voicemail passwords. She coached Bonnie on how to log into his Sprint account online and set up a username and password. That way she'll be able to just reset his voicemail pin online.

"Girl, what if he already has an account online?" Bonnie asked.

"Chile please! Niggas don't ever go online to set that shit up," Monique said, laughing.

"Ok cool. I'm gon' set it up now," Bonnie said.

After setting up the online profile she was able to reset his password to the last 4-digits of his cell phone number. She waited until she knew he was at the gym to call him so that he wouldn't answer.

*You have ten new messages, to listen you your messages press 1…*Bonnie anxiously skipped through all of the voicemails until she heard a female's voice. *This is my last time calling you since I've been calling you for a week straight and you haven't returned any of my calls. I should've known better than to fuck with you anyway. You be on the same time these other nut ass niggas be on. So I'm cool on you too. Just wanted to let you know you's a lame and if you ain't wanna talk to me anymore after you got what you wanted then you should've been a man about that shit.*

Bonnie wrote down the number before skipping to the next message. The same chick left two other messages a few days prior, ranting on about how he was ignoring her phone calls. "This is too much. Hell, I should've just stayed with Karl's ass," Bonnie said out loud to herself while dialing the anonymous chick's number.

"Hello," the girl answered.

"Hey, this is Bonnie. T's girlfriend."

"Yeah and? Why the hell are you calling me?" she asked,

in a nasty tone.

Bonnie knew if she snapped back at this chick, she wouldn't get anywhere. The last thing she wanted was for the girl to hang up. So, she put her game face on and manipulated the hell out of her.

"Listen, I'm not calling you with any drama. It's not my style," she said, in a calm voice. "I know that you've been messing with my man. I asked him about you and he said you were nobody, just a lil' hood rat from around the way." Bonnie was trying to get her so irritated she would tell everything. Especially, since she was already heated he hit it and quit it.

"I've been messing with T for a couple months now," she said. I don't know why he would try to play me. Hell, I know too much."

"So you knew he had a girl?" Bonnie questioned.

"Yeah I knew. He told me he had a girl and that ya'll was about to have a baby. He told me everything. There were times when you called and he was in front of me," she said.

"Have ya'll gone out together?"

"Yeah we went bowling and shit like that." Bonnie had a flashback to the time when she called him and he told her he was out bowling with his homeys.

"Did ya'll fuck?"

"Yeah we did…a couple of times."

"Did ya'll use a condom?"

"The first time we did, but every time after that no," she said. Bonnie was beyond disgusted. She wondered if this was the nasty bitch who'd given him Gonorrhea.

"When is the last time ya'll fucked?"

"Yesterday," she said, lying through her teeth.

"Well thank you for telling me all I need to know. Just one more thing before I go. What's your name?"

"Malaysia," she said.

Bonnie said thank you, and then hung up. She knew Malaysia lied about some things, especially when she said they had sex the day before. She just heard the chick say on his answering machine she hadn't reached him all week. Still, she knew a lot of what she said, had some truth to it.

She didn't call Ted's phone this time. She sat on the sofa in the living room all night, patiently waited for him to come home. When Bonnie heard him turn the key in the lock, she stood up facing the door so that she could confront him. She didn't let him take two steps before screaming out, "I talked to your bitch Malaysia. I know every fucking thing!" Ted just stood there with a shocked expression on his face.

"Is that the nasty bitch you got a disease from? She told me ya'll been fucking raw."

"That bitch lying. I never fucked her. All she did was suck my dick."

"You're a liar Ted. You took that bitch bowling and shit!" she screamed. "I can't even believe you fucked this bitch without a condom. Damn, if you gon' fuck on me at least have enough respect to strap up!"

"I said I didn't fuck her," he said. "I'm about to call that bitch."

"Call her and put it on speaker," Bonnie said, with one hand on her hip.

When Malaysia answered the phone, he immediately went in on her.

"Bitch why you lie and tell my girl we fucked, when all you did was suck my dick. You just mad cause I been duckin' your nut ass!" Ted screamed.

Malaysia was spitting words back at him, but Ted was purposely raising his voice to over talk her. He didn't want her to throw anything out there that would further piss Bonnie off.

"Fuck outta here you nut ass bitch! And stop calling my phone!"

Bonnie heard Ted clearly say to Malaysia she only gave him oral, still she felt he was lying. She knew Ted would do and say anything to make her believe otherwise. And this entire ordeal made Bonnie look at him completely different but she was ready to let it go and move on. She had bigger things to focus on. Like the arrival of her baby boy.

When Bonnie was nine months and close to her due date, Karen flew out to Philly to be with her. She didn't want to miss the birth of her first grandchild for nothing in the world. Bonnie was expected to go in labor on November 19, 2009, but at Bonnie's last doctor's visit she was told the baby was already weighing in at eight pounds and she may have to be induced. Hearing the word induced was like music to Bonnie's ears. Her last month of pregnancy was the worst! The weeks seemed to drag, and between the back pains, swollen ankles and constant heart burn, Bonnie was miserable. But Karen knew better. She told Bonnie the last thing she wanted was to be induced. She said it would be less painful if she went in naturally.

So, they went online and googled "ways to bring on labor at home." There were all sorts of advice on self-induced labor, but Bonnie settled for good ol' fashion sex and nipple stimulation to help bring on the contractions. Fortunately for Bonnie she didn't have to be induced. Around six in the morning, she started to feel contractions. By eight o' clock, the contractions became very intense and she knew it was time.

Ted and Karen rushed Bonnie to Abington Memorial Hospital. The doctors ran test to make sure it wasn't a false labor. After about a half hour, they were told Bonnie would be admitted and she would be soon having a baby.

Before Bonnie was even given a room, the nurse was already asking her if she wanted an epidural. She was doing pretty well with the contractions and was thinking to herself, *this isn't as bad as I thought it would be*…but the nurse warned her if she waited too late, she wouldn't be able to get it. So, she decided to get the epidural. The anesthesiologist told Bonnie to sit up, put her head down and not to move. His exact words, "It's imperative that you're very still during this procedure." He told her she could be paralyzed if she moved during the injection.

The epidural took effect instantly and Bonnie couldn't

feel anything from the waist down. The doctors weren't happy with her labor progression, so they broke her water and gave her shots of Pitocin to help bring on stronger contractions.

A few hours later, Bonnie started to feel intense cramps and anal pressure. It felt like something was going to fall out of her butt. She yelled out, "This epidural wore off, I can feel everything now!" The nurse came over and placed something cold on Bonnie's thigh and asked her if she could feel it. She said, "no, but I can feel something ripping through me! Please go get the doctor!" The nurse dismissed her at first and told her what she felt was normal. Bonnie gave her the most vicious look that anyone could give and told her, "No go get the fucking doctor!" She didn't know what was irking her more, the dippy ass nurse or the fact, Ted was sitting there on his cell phone holding a normal conversation, while she was in the worst possible pain.

The doctor came into the room and checked Bonnie. She looked at the nurse and said, "She's ready. She's fully dilated." The nurse looked at Bonnie with an embarrassed look on her face and apologized for not being more thorough. The nurse and the doctors quickly got prepared and positioned Bonnie's bed to prepare for delivery.

The nurse motioned for Ted to come over and help. The nurse held Bonnie's left leg, while Ted held her right. All she heard was "Push…Push…he's coming fast! You can do it…Come on…Push!" Then she started to feel a burning sensation, the pain was indescribable. "Get it out now!" she screamed. And less than one minute later, she pushed out a beautiful baby boy with a head full of sandy brown hair. All Bonnie heard was Ted's voice saying he wanted to cut the umbilical cord.

Bonnie didn't even reach out to grab him. She fell back on the bed and exhaled, with her eyes still closed. She was just relieved it was over and when she heard him cry she knew he was alright. They took the baby to be cleaned, weighed, measured and checked. He was a perfectly healthy boy, weighing in at eight pounds and ten ounces. Ted had two other children but he wasn't present for their births, so this was a very proud moment for him. He stood over his baby son, talking to him and taking pictures.

The nurse wrapped him in a blanket and handed him over to Bonnie. He was such a beautiful baby boy and there was no way Ted could deny him. The only thing Bonnie had given him were her tight almond shaped eyes. Other than that he looked identical to Ted. Holding him in her arms sent warmth through her heart and she instantly fell in love with him. She looked at Ted sitting next to her and all the regret, doubt, and confusion went out of the window. Bonnie believed that everything happens for a reason, and there was a reason why she was sitting there with Ted, and not Karl. And no matter what was yet to come, she was thankful for her precious gift...Sean Michael Pitts.

CHAPTER THIRTEEN
Emotional Rollercoaster

The first two weeks of being home with Sean, Bonnie was a mess. She didn't get any proper sleep since she left the hospital. He woke up every two hours for a bottle, and was already very spoiled. All he wanted was for Bonnie to hold him. If and whenever she would put him down he would scream from the top of his lungs. Bonnie would be so sleepy til' she would fall asleep with him lying on her chest. She would get up in the middle of the night like clockwork to warm his bottles. She got absolutely zero help from Ted, which made her more conflicted emotionally. She didn't understand why he didn't want to help out more, especially after seeing how stressed she was. He even had the audacity to wake Bonnie up out of her sleep one night, just to tell her that the baby was crying.

Bonnie grew so frustrated with Ted's negligence as a partner that she barely spoke to him at home. Monique and Tess helped out as much as they could which wasn't a lot because they both worked full-time jobs and had other obligations. Bonnie cried many nights wishing she could just shut her eyes and get a full eight hours of sleep.

But after a month, things started to get a lot easier for

Bonnie. She and Sean settled into a routine that worked for the both of them. He took longer naps, which allowed her to get more rest as well. As hard as it was for Bonnie, she stopped picking him up and holding him all day like she used to, no matter how loud he would cry. Her mother told her, "Girl if he's dry and fed and not sick, there is nothing wrong with letting that baby cry. Stop spoiling him." So, that's exactly what she did and it worked out in her favor. He was now more independent and okay with sitting in his bouncer or being in his swing.

During this time, Bonnie was getting a lot of offers to do different music videos and magazines but she turned them all down. She wasn't interested in returning back to the urban modeling world, and she was over the whole vixen thing. But she was grateful for the fans she gained because of it. She was doing so well with selling her book independently she signed a deal with a well-known publishing company, based in New York City. She re-released "Shadow of a Gold digger" and it was moving off the shelves like crazy.

Now, Bonnie was focused on shedding all of the baby weight. She would be dammed if she would become one of those, *used to be bad bitches*. She ran on the eighteen hundred dollar Nautilus Mobia Treadmill Ted bought her and made sure she did tons of squats and crunches to tone everything back up. A lot of the weight was just water weight anyway and she lost it rapidly. Bonnie was determined to get her sexy back and she did. Just when she felt as though she was getting back into the groove of things, she received a phone call that shook her entire world.

It was May 10, 2010, when Ted called Bonnie and said, "I just saw Karl." And when he said the words, "He's home," Bonnie felt a rush of emotions.

"Really? What happened?" Bonnie asked.

"He called me and said he wanted to meet up with me so we can talk. So, I met him on his mom's block."

"Yeah," Bonnie said, anxiously waiting for the details.

"He said, he's not mad anymore about what happened

with me and you. He was hurt for a long time more than anything and now he's moved on," Ted said. "He introduced me to his new girl and everything...some chick named Vicky."

Wow Bonnie thought to herself. Hearing those words hurt Bonnie to her heart. She couldn't believe he was still with her. And she couldn't believe Karl was really home. All of the feelings she hid deep down inside, began surfacing again. But Ted intentionally withheld one important piece of information...He asked where she was and when Ted told Karl he and Bonnie were still together, there was no denying the hurt in Karl's eyes.

Karl still loved Bonnie and he planned on finding her and making things right. He was willing to start over and leave the past behind them but knowing she was still with Ted changed everything.

He cared for Vicky and was appreciative of her. She helped him through one of the most difficult times in his life. He truly believed Bonnie was his payback for every time he mistreated a woman in his life. Bonnie stripped him of everything and broke him down as a man. Vicky was there to pick up the pieces and for the remaining two years of his sentence she carried him when he couldn't carry himself. But not even that was enough to make him fall in love with her. No matter how hard he tried he just couldn't.

When Bonnie hung up the phone with Ted she called Mahanoy prison to find out when he was released. The guard told her he was just released that morning and he would be staying at Kintock Halfway house on East Erie Avenue, in Philadelphia. Bonnie immediately went on the internet to get their phone number. She desperately needed to talk to him. She wanted to hear his voice but she didn't know how he would react. She didn't know if he would curse her out, and then tell Ted she called him so she prepared herself for the worse. She slipped on her clothes and ran to Walmart to buy a prepaid cell phone. That way she could deny it if Karl did tell Ted she called. He wouldn't have Bonnie's number to back up his claims.

Once she got her prepaid phone she called the halfway house and asked for Karl Atkins. She was transferred to his case worker and was told his curfew wasn't until nine p.m. He asked her if she wanted to leave a message. Her first thought was not to leave a message, but she did anyway. And why the words, "Tell him to call his wife Bonnie," left Bonnie's mouth, she didn't understood why. She left her phone number and hung up the phone thinking, *what the hell did I just do? I'm playing with fire right now.*

At nine o' five on the dot, Bonnie's prepaid phone rang. Her heart started pounding really fast. No one else had the number so she knew it was Karl calling. She didn't expect to hear back from him so soon. The moment Karl's case worker handed him the note to call Bonnie, he anxiously walked to his room to call her.

"Hello," she answered, nervously.

"What's up Bonnie? I just got your message," he said.

"I just wanted to talk to you and see how you were doing."

"I'm alright B. I'm just glad to be home."

"Well, I'm glad you're home too. I want you to know that I still care about you and I want nothing but the best for you," she said.

"Oh word? You want nothing but the best for me but you still with my man B," he said. "Let me ask you something…how old is the baby?"

"He's six months," she said, in a low tone.

"Wow. That shit crazy," he said. "I can't believe you Bonnie. You fucked us up."

"You can't just put everything on me Karl. You did wrong too."

"But at least we could've came back from that shit though B! I could've fixed us. I was gon' come home and make up for all that shit. Tell me how and the fuck we gon' come back from this? You fucked my man and had a baby by him!" he said, raising his voice. Bonnie could hear the anger building up inside of him.

"I know Karl. I'm sorry," she said. "I never meant to hurt you."

"That's bullshit Bonnie. You told me you was gon' get me back and you did. You destroyed me while I was in jail. I was in there fucked up. You know how many times I wished that you would just pop up and see me, or even write me? You left me for dead in there!"

"Karl we both hurt each other. I didn't contact you in hopes of us getting back together. I just want to..."
Something about hearing that set Karl off.

"Fuck you Bitch! We can never get back together. You with my man! You turned out to be the worst kind of fucking woman! A good girl gone bad. You're just like your mother. You ain't shit Bonnie!" Bonnie couldn't bear to hear any more of the harsh words that fired from Karl's mouth. She hung up the phone and tears began pouring from her eyes. If there was anyone that knew how to hit Bonnie where it hurt, it was Karl. She felt like the biggest piece of shit in the world after talking to him and she regretted ever reaching out.

The entire day, Bonnie was nervous as hell thinking she would eventually get a call from Ted cursing her out about contacting Karl. She knew this day would come, but she had no idea she would be hurting so badly because of it. She tried to remind herself of all the terrible things he'd done to her throughout their relationship. Bonnie told herself over and over again she wasn't in love with Karl anymore. *Maybe it's just a phase I'm going through right now because he just came home. I'll be over this shit in no time.* She desperately needed to put her mind and heart at ease. And if lying to herself would do the trick...then she was all for it.

To Bonnie's surprise Karl didn't mention anything to Ted about their conversation. This confused her so bad to the point she called her mother for some insight. Karen told Bonnie the only reason he didn't tell Ted, was because he didn't want it to be their last time talking. And boy was she right. Karl called Bonnie's phone the very next day. She kept the phone hidden in her closet and tucked away in an old Gucci pocketbook. When she looked at her phone she saw Karl called her five times, and even left a voicemail saying, "Bonnie I'm sorry I snapped on you. Please give me a call." So, she did and this time their conversation was much more pleasant.

"Hey Karl."

"Hey B. I'm sorry I was tripping on you. You gotta understand I'm still hurt over this shit. You can't possibly think I'm okay with you being with him."

"Didn't you tell him you were okay with it and you've moved on?"

"Yeah I told him that. For a while I was mad as shit. All I wanted to do was come home and get revenge on that nigga, but after a while I said fuck it. She chose. He ain't put a gun to your head and make you fuck him."

"I want you to know, we weren't messing around all that time, if that's what you're thinking. It didn't happen until we broke up."

"C'mon B. Stop it. I don't believe you," he said. "And it doesn't matter. What matters is that you still with this nigga. Every day you wake up to him, you're disrespecting me. Remember that." Bonnie just held the phone in complete silence.

"I will never co-sign that shit! You don't belong with him! I found you. I had you when you was young and all that. I taught you everything you know."

"I know Karl and I'll always love you because of that."

"You messed up my life. We were supposed to move to Atlanta, do this book shit together and get this money. I don't wanna be here Bonnie. I feel like I'm gon' die in these streets of Philly."

"Don't say that Karl. Regardless of what you may think, I don't know what I'd do if something ever happened to you."

"If you care about me that much, then you need to leave him alone. Show me that you love me...leave him and I'll forgive you. That's my word," he said, in a firm voice.

"Do you still love me Karl?"

"I'm gon' love you til' the day I die Bonnie." Hearing Karl say those words made Bonnie's heart skip a beat.

"Damn Karl I hate things had to turn out this way. It wasn't supposed to be like this," she said.

They stayed on the phone for over an hour, just talking about their love and what could've been. Without a doubt, Karl still loved Bonnie, in spite of what she did to him but he felt conflicted. A huge part of him wanted to just take her away from Philly and start over but then another part of him despised her. How could they ever really escape their past? He would forever be reminded of the pain and embarrassment she caused him every time he laid eyes on her son.

A couple of months passed, and although Bonnie and Karl were communicating back and forth over the phone, he'd been begging to see her in person. As badly as she wanted to see him she was still afraid he would tell Ted. Especially since he'd been up and down with his feelings towards her. He would tell her he loved her one day and then the next day he would be cursing her out, calling her all types of bitches and whores.

Everyone told Bonnie to stay away from Karl, especially her mother Karen. She said, "Bonnie you need to leave him alone. He's never going to forgive you for having a baby on him." And Monique and Tess were convinced he was only out to get some sort of evil revenge. "Girl that nigga don't want to see you with Ted. He's gon' wait until he has enough on your ass and then he's gonna expose you. Don't trust him!" is what they said. Bonnie didn't know what to believe. When she heard him say he loved her she felt it was real. And during those nasty arguments when he told her he hated her...she felt it was real as well. So, she played it safe. She made excuses for why she couldn't see him. This only made Karl more angry with her because he was no fool. He knew Ted was the reason she stayed away. Eventually, Bonnie had enough of Karl's emotional rollercoaster ride. She got rid of her "creep phone," leaving Karl with no way to contact her.

A few months later, Bonnie logged into her Facebook account and saw she had a pending friend request from "KarlthewriterAtkins" She immediately clicked ignore, *Fuck is he sending me a friend request for if he hates me so much*! Bonnie thought to herself. *That nigga just tryna be nosey!* she said, as she scrolled through her other pending request. She couldn't help but navigate her way back to Karl's page to do a little bit of spying herself. As she scrolled through his page, she came across a picture of him and some chick with the caption "Me and my baby." Then she saw several pictures of him and the same chick. Bonnie didn't know who she was but it definitely wasn't Vicky. Learning that he and Vicky were no longer together brought a huge smile across Bonnie's face. But now she was curious to know who this new bitch was and she was going to find out.

Bonnie blocked her number out by dialing *67, and then dialed Karl's number.

"Hello?"

"Hey Karl," she said. "How are you?"

"Bonnie?"

"Yeah." Hearing Bonnie's voice made him feel warm inside.

"I'm good B. How are you?"

"I'm okay," she said.

"That's good to hear. I've been thinking about you."

"I think about you all the time Karl."

"How's your son doing?"

"He's doing good. Thanks for asking," she said. "So what have you been up to?"

"I just been staying focused and out of trouble. I opened up a detail shop, just finished up my book and I'm about to release it next month. I'm real excited about that."

"Wow! That's great Karl. I'm really happy for you!" she said, excitedly.

"Thanks B."

"Are you in a relationship right now?" she asked.

"Naw not really. I'm seeing somebody but it's nothing serious," he responded.

"What happened with you and Vicky?" she pried.

"She was never my type but I tried to make it work on the strength she was a good person and she was there for me. But shit, she was just too bland for me. She didn't even turn me on sexually."

"So you left her because she was boring? That's something ya'll could've worked on," she said, pretending to show concern about their breakup. Deep down inside she was feeling like, *that's what that bitch get for being so damn thirsty. Trying to step in and take what's mine. Nigga came home and left your ass.*

"It is what it is. She just didn't make me happy," he said. "Can I ask you a question?"

"Sure. You can ask me anything," she said.

"Are you happy B?"

"Yes, I'm happy."

"Fuck outta here. C'mon B, it's me. I know you ain't happy with that nigga," he said.

"You asked me if I was happy. You didn't ask me if I was happy with him."

"Are you happy with him?"

"I don't feel comfortable talking about that with you. I don't wanna talk about him," she said.

"You ain't gotta answer it. I know it kills you that we're not together right now."

"I wouldn't say that it kills me, but sometimes I do wish that things were different."

Bonnie would go days…sometimes weeks without calling him and when she did she would always call private. Not having a number to reach her drove him crazy, and no matter how many times he said he wouldn't answer her blocked calls, he would pick up anyway. This went on for months between the two of them. He desperately wanted to see her and it burned him up she was being so loyal to Ted.

He didn't understand it. How could she be riding for him so hard? He got mad once and told her, "You ain't mines no more! You his bitch now! And even though Karl felt Ted wasn't on his level or of his caliber, losing Bonnie to him made him feel inadequate.

Since Karl came home he jumped from woman to woman. He always found something in them he didn't like. Or maybe it was the fact he was searching for someone that reminded him of Bonnie. He thought if he could find someone who could give him what Bonnie gave him, then he could finally move on with his life and be happy. Unfortunately for Karl, he hadn't met that person and inside he longed for another "B".

CHAPTER FOURTEEN
Everything I Miss at Home

It was the beginning of Summer, and the weather was hot and scorching on this day. Ted was cruising the streets of South Philly in his new black Maserati with the top dropped, blasting Kanye and Jay Z's "Niggas in Paris." The attention given whenever he brought his eye candy out made him feel like a hood celebrity. People would stop and stare in amazement because he was pushing the same whip as Dr. Dre and other major celebrities. Ted wasn't as flashy as Karl and some other cats when it came to all the jewelry and mink coats, but when it came to his cars and bank rolls nobody could stand next to him.

Ted pulled over on 23rd and Morris St, when he spotted his homey Dawul standing on the corner talking to one of his boys.

"Alright I'll be sure to get up with you playboy! Asalam Alaikum!" Dawul yelled out to his boy, as he hopped into his car.

He turned his attention to Ted with a big smile on his face. They put up their fist, and threw playful jabs like they always did. Then they embraced in a brief hug.

"That bitch is bad!" Dawul said, referring to his Maserati.

"You know how I do…I keep a bad bitch!" Ted said, while chuckling.

"Damn is that Asia over there on the porch?" Ted asked. He knew Asia from around the way but he hadn't seen her in years. The last time he seen her she was about eighteen, scrawny and timid. But looking at her now he saw a sexy, voluptuous woman that he wouldn't mind laying down. Yes, Ted did him from time to time. Still, he spoke very highly of Bonnie to niggas and bitches. He was quick to pull out his phone and show them pictures of his girl and he wasn't afraid to let a chick know how much he loved her. But just like most men, no matter how pretty his woman is…if they have a weakness for bad bitches then they'll forever be on the prowl. A man doesn't sit down until he's ready to sit down. Only he knows when he's done playing.

Ted walked over to the bottom of the step and called Asia down. He stared at her thick legs, and 38 D breast as she walked down the steps. She was wearing shorts so short they would qualify as coochie cutters, a white tank top that she cut in half to expose her entire belly and cheap sandals from Barefeet Shoes. Asia felt like a contestant on the price is right as she approached Ted. She knew Ted had a lot of bread and seeing him pull up in a Maserati made her pussy wet.

"What's up T," she said, with one hand on her hip.

"You," he said, flirting.

"Oh really?"

"Yup. What's your number?" he said, pulling his cell phone out of his pocket.

"2674320021," she said.

"Alright I'ma text you so you can lock me in. Maybe we can get together later."

"Okay baby. Hit me up," she said.

Chicken heads like Asia didn't require much of a conversation, they made it way too easy. Ted gave Dawul a hand shake, jumped into his whip and sped off. He didn't waste any time getting back at her. He texted her less than twenty minutes later, saying *you look good as shit. I need that*. She responded back *lol okay*, smiling from ear to ear. They texted each other back and forth all day. He told her to send him a freaky picture and she obliged, sending him a picture of her lying on the bed, with her legs spread and pulling her panties to the side. Her exposed hairy pussy got Ted rock hard instantly. *You gon' let me taste it?* he texted. *Yup. When you want to?* she responded. *Tonight, Ted texted back. Okay,* she replied.

Ted anxiously hung around South Philly, waiting for Asia to get back to him. She was supposed to call him at eight, so he could pick her up. He planned on getting a room and wearing her ass out for an hour or so. Ten o' clock arrived and he still hadn't heard from her. He texted her, *What you gon' do?* she replied back, *I'm not able to get a baby sitter.* Ted was so irked that he didn't even respond. He got into his car and headed home. When he got home Bonnie was already asleep. He took off all his clothes, climbed in bed with her, and held her close from the side. She awoke when she felt him sliding her panties down. She went underneath the covers and began sucking his dick like her life depended on it. He moaned in pleasure. Bonnie then climbed on top of him and rode him, making his eyes roll in the back of his head. They had their usual wild passionate sex all night long, before falling to sleep in each other's arms.

The next morning while Ted was in the shower, Bonnie decided to do a little snooping. Ted's phone was so hard to get to these days and she had that gut feeling he was hiding something. They had many arguments about him hiding his phone from her, leaving it in the car or tucked away in the house somewhere. But on this particular morning he slipped up and left his phone on the side of the bed. When Bonnie spotted it on the floor she lit up inside, as if she found a pot of gold.

She didn't worry too much about his call log. Nowadays, people barely talked over the phone. You were able to hold an entire conversation through a text, so Bonnie went directly to his text mail. The first name she saw when she opened the folder was the name Asia and there were fifty four messages between them. She opened the message and scrolled to the beginning of the thread, and read each and every message word from word. When Bonnie saw the picture of Asia's pussy she was disgusted, but seeing that Ted asked her if he could taste it really set Bonnie on fire.

Still half naked, Bonnie rushed into the bathroom heated, blood boiling and ready for war. She aggressively pulled back the shower curtain and pushed him so hard, he fell backwards.

"You ain't shit nigga!" she yelled at him.

"What? What are you talkin' about?" he asked, with a frightened look on his face. He looked at Bonnie's hand and saw that she was holding his cell phone and he knew exactly what she was talking about.

"I saw the text messages Ted! You're so fucking nasty! I can't believe you were telling this bitch you wanted to taste her pussy!"

"I didn't touch that girl," he said.

"Yeah that's because the ratchet ass bitch couldn't get a babysitter! Don't try and play me like I'm stupid!" she screamed.

Bonnie slammed his cell phone against the wall, causing it to shatter into pieces.

"Look what you did! You broke my fucking phone!"

"So what! Go buy another one!" She stormed out of the bathroom and he quickly followed behind her, butt ass naked.

"Why are you always starting with me Bonnie?"

"Are you serious? Why are you always cheating? I ain't never have to put up with this kind of shit!"

"You're right cause he was too busy whooping your fucking ass!" he spat.

"Don't you dare throw that shit in my face. He never brought home no fucking diseases," she said. "You just running around here reckless and shit."

"Man I don't have time for this shit," he said, turning his back to walk away.

"Well leave then! Go call that bitch Asia and see if she'll let you suck on her nasty pussy!"

Ted wanted out of the house and away from Bonnie as soon as possible. He dressed in a hurry and left without saying a word. Bonnie sat on the edge of her bed fuming inside. Her mind started racing…*I can't believe I left Karl for this shit!* She picked up her cell phone and dialed Karl's number only to find out his number changed. She signed into her face book account and sent him a message saying "hey." She anxiously waited for a reply, checking her phone every couple of minutes for the Facebook notification. When Karl's message appeared on her screen she lit up.

"Hey B. Funny that you messaged me because I was just thinking of you."

"Really?"

I always think about you. Where are we supposed to be right now?"

"Atlanta." She smiled, as she wrote back.

"Yup. Me and you."

"Do you ever feel like you wanna just get up and go?"

"All the time. Call me I would love to hear you voice. 2155541117."

"Okay I will."

Bonnie sat there and contemplated on whether or not she should call. Twenty minutes later she received another message from Karl.

"I'm waiting…"

Fuck it. She dialed Karl's number and this time she didn't block her number. She didn't care what got back to Ted at this point. She was tired of him taking her love for granted. Karl was thrilled Bonnie actually let her number show this time. They talked for hours, catching up on what was going on in each other's lives. He just had a breakup but this was no real news to Bonnie. He told Bonnie he really wanted to see her and without any hesitation Bonnie agreed to meeting him. It had been three years since they'd seen each other and she wanted to make sure she looked better than he remembered. She wore white leggings, a white tank top, gold Christian Louboutins, and gold accessories to bring out her shoes. She put her hair on top of her head in a bun, the way she used to wear it back in the day.

Karl called Bonnie at six o'clock and told her to come outside. Sitting on her dad's block waiting for her to come out brought back many good memories. When Bonnie came walking down the steps and to his car, Karl could feel his heart racing.

"Hey baby," she said, with a warm smile on her face.

"Hey B," he said. "Damn you're so fucking pretty."

"Thank you, you look good too."

She reached over and gave him a hug. Just when she was about to pull back, he pulled her closer.

"It feels so good to have you in my arms right now," he said, before exhaling.

"I really missed you Karl."

"I missed you too. I still love you Bonnie," he said. "After all that's happened, I still love you.

"I love you too Karl. That will never change."

Karl drove around the corner to Belfield Park. He changed the station to 105.3, cranked the volume and rolled the windows down, so they could hear the music blazing through the speakers of his Cadillac DTS. "Have me anyway you want to, just take care and love me til' my tension's gone. Cause you are my starship, come take me up tonight and don't be late, and don't you come too soon…"

"Oh that's my song!" Bonnie said, excitedly.

"You're such an old soul," he said. "I always loved that about you." Bonnie just smiled.

Karl sat on the top of a bench table and Bonnie sat below him in between his legs. They both felt right at home with one another, as they sat close talking for hours. After everything they'd been through there was no denying the love was still there. The feeling Karl gave her, she didn't get from Ted or any other man for that matter. And for Karl no other woman could keep his attention the way that she could. He felt incomplete without her…and in that moment, he finally felt whole again.

Every night after that, they talked every day…first thing in the morning and before they went to bed at night. His spot up City Line Avenue became a regular chill spot for Bonnie. They would order take out and watch Netflix movies all day long. He was finally able to do all of the things he wished he would've done when they were together. He never stayed in and watched movies with her or spent any real quality time. Now, all he wanted was to show Bonnie a different side to him. A better side.

"Bonnie you're one bold bitch!" Monique said, as she, Tess and Bonnie walked into Saks Fifth Avenue on City Line Avenue. For the first time, Bonnie regretted opening her mouth to her girlfriends. *I should've kept my fucking my mouth shut* she thought to herself. Bonnie removed her oversized butterfly shaped Chanel sunglasses from her face and placed them on top of her head. She spotted a pair of crystal-coated platform pumps by Giuseppe Zanotti.

"I need these in my life. These bitches are bad!" Bonnie said, trying to divert the conversation.

"Yes bitch, Shoeicide!" Monique said. "But don't be tryna change the subject."

"I know right!" Tess chimed in. "Do you even know what you're doing?"

"Ya'll need to relax. Hell, we ain't fucking." Bonnie said, in her defense.

"Not yet bitch! And even if ya'll don't, you still playing with fire girl!" Tess said.

"We've been in contact on and off for a whole year and he never ran his mouth."

"Cause he don't have enough on you yet, but you better believe it...Karl wants revenge," Monique said.

"She's right B. You need to cut him off before you get yourself in too deep."

"I got this ya'll. I know what I'm doing. Besides, I wouldn't even be talking to Karl if Ted wasn't fucking up."

"Listen girl, I'm not saying don't do you. But don't you think it's dangerous messing around with Karl?" Monique said.

"Maybe, but I still love Karl and If he's not concerned then neither am I," Bonnie said. But she was concerned. She tried her best to disguise it but truthfully Bonnie knew she was playing a dangerous game. Only problem was, she wasn't ready to throw in her hand yet.

"Can I get these in a size eight please?" Bonnie said to the blonde sales woman.

"And these in a size six," Monique said, referring to a pair of Gucci sandals.

Tess looked at Monique and Bonnie and sucked her teeth. "Ya'll bitches ain't right. Ya'll know I'm broke and just rubbing it in my damn face."

They all laughed. "It's cool though. I get paid next week and I'm back in here," Tess said, while chuckling.

"Oh shit I'm gon' be late. I gotta hurry up and get back to work," Monique said.

"I need to get going too, I have to go in at 3:30," Tess said.

The three of them embraced in a hug and told each other they would talk later. Bonnie called Karl to let him know she was in the area and wanted to see him. When he gave her the okay, Bonnie started speeding and anxiously maneuvering her way through all of the traffic. "Move bitch! Go around!" Bonnie yelled at a driver who was patiently waiting behind a Septa bus. Bonnie sped up and went around both the driver and bus, while giving the young girl the middle finger. She picked up her crazy driving skills and road rage from none one other than Karl. Bonnie couldn't wait to see her boo. Whenever she was around him, he would light up her entire world. The feeling was truly indescribable.

"Sexy Sexy!" Karl yelled from the top of the balcony, as he watched Bonnie walk up the steps to his apartment. He came down to meet her, wearing nothing but gym shorts and a pair of Jordan's.

"B you one bad muthafucka!" Karl said. "These bitches out here ain't got shit on you." Bonnie smiled and gave him a look like *yeah I know nigga.*

The moment they stepped foot inside Karl's apartment, they were kissing and touching all over each other. He gripped Bonnie's round ass in the palm of his hand. "Damn this ass fat as shit." He said. Bonnie turned around and started shaking her ass on him, making him rock hard. "Hahaha, let me stop playing before it go down in here," she said jokingly. She turned around and faced Karl, he wrapped his arms around her and squeezed real tight before releasing her.

"You know I want you back right?"

"You do?" she asked, with a sparkle in her eyes.

"I do B. You make me happy," he said. "It ain't no other woman that can make me feel the way you do."

"I feel the same way. It's just that I don't wanna cause no problems," she said.

"What problems you gon' cause? B, you mines, you always been mines. What the fuck that nigga gon' say to me?" he said, with a devilish grin on his face.

"I'm just saying…" Bonnie couldn't even finish her sentence.

"Listen, deep down inside he knows that I'm gon' take you back. You don't belong with that nigga you and him don't even make sense."

"Do you really think we can be happy together after all that's happened?" she asked.

"I took you through so much shit and you loved me still. Hell, you caught me in bed with a bitch, I put my hands on you and all types of nut shit and you forgave me. So how can I not forgive you for this one mistake?"

Bonnie stared into his eyes and she could feel his sincerity. This was no bullshit, he meant every word. But in the back of her mind she could hear all the voices telling her not to trust him, he just wants revenge and that he'll never be able to accept her son. She grabbed his hand, put it up to her mouth and kissed it gently like she used to. She knew how to send chills through Karl's entire body with one single kiss or touch. He had a thing for Bonnie and there was nothing that anyone could do or say to change it.

"I just need to know that you're all in. I'll talk to that nigga man to man and let him know what it is," he said. "I'ma tell that nigga thanks for looking out, but I got her from here on out," he said, while laughing.

"You stupid," she said with a giggle.

Bonnie got down on her knees and pulled down Karl's shorts. She stuck her tongue out at him real nasty the way he always told her to, and he instantly became hard as a brick. She licked all over his dick, slowly, and paying attention to every inch before taking all of him into her mouth and down her throat. He kept pushing her head down further and further, while moaning in ecstasy. "C'mon cum in my fucking mouth," she said to him. This usually got him every time but Karl was tired of Bonnie just giving him head and no pussy. In her mind, as long as she hadn't actually fucked him yet, he didn't really have anything on her. But Karl was no fool, he needed to know where they stood and where her head was at.

"This don't mean shit to me Bonnie. I want that pussy," he said.

"Let's just wait," she said. "I'm not ready."

"What you mean you not ready? I ain't tryna hear that shit."

Karl grabbed Bonnie, took her into his bedroom, and started ripping her clothes off. He went into his dresser drawer and grabbed a magnum condom. "Take that shit off." he said. Bonnie didn't put up much of a fight this time. She took off all her clothes and laid on the bed with her legs spread wide open. Karl climbed on top of her and Bonnie wrapped her arms around him, pulling him close to her. He slid his hard, ten inch dick inside her wet pussy and started thrusting it in and out. Bonnie's eyes rolled in the back of her head as he pounded her. "You been missing me inside you huh? This pussy wet as shit for daddy," he said. "Yes I've missed you!" she screamed out. Karl stopped and pulled the condom off his dick. "You my bitch. This my pussy," he said. "Now sit on this big dick and ride me like I taught you!" he said, aggressively. Bonnie climbed on top of him and began twerking and bouncing her ass while riding him. She could feel him getting harder and harder inside of her. She groaned in pain mixed with pleasure. Karl wrapped both hands around her neck gently squeezing, as she bounced up and down on his hard dick. "That nigga don't fuck you like this! He don't know how you like to be fucked!" he said, as he choked her. He flipped her over and started hitting it hard from behind. His mind started racing, and he started having visions of Bonnie being intimate with Ted, which made him pump even harder. Bonnie began to scream, he was pounding her so hard. "I'm about to bust!" he said. Bonnie started throwing her ass back harder, "Yeah cum in this pussy baby," she said, making Karl lose all control and explode inside of her.

It had been years since Bonnie had been fucked liked that. Although she and Ted had a pretty good sex life, it was nothing compared to the wild, crazy sex she and Karl shared. They jumped in the shower together and washed up. They took turns washing each other's backs like they used to, and in that moment it seemed as though everything was fine. Like nothing of the past ever existed. Nothing or no one else mattered to them. It felt just like the old days, when it was just Karl and Bonnie against the world.

Now that Bonnie and Karl was on again she wasn't feeling her home situation. In her mind, she would come up with so many reasons why she should be with Karl over Ted. Spending time with Karl opened her eyes to everything she was missing at home. With Karl everyday was like an adventure. He was always fun and spontaneous. She missed going out to the club with her man, both of them looking good and shutting shit down. Or how she used to dress up in her sexy lingerie and dance for him, while he held the camcorder. Oh and how could she forget about the countless homemade porno flicks she and Karl made together. Ted would never be into that sort of thing. He was much more conservative, wasn't the going out type and wouldn't take a drink if someone paid him to. A night of fun for him was going the movies, out to eat or just maybe a trip to AC every now and then. Bonnie told herself she and Karl were soul mates, and that they belonged together. There was an unexplainable chemistry between the two of them ever since day one and Bonnie was convinced that no one could lift the hold he had on her heart.

It was Bonnie's twenty-fifth birthday, and Ted surprised her with a brand new 2011 Ranger Rover. It was white, with peanut butter interior and light tinted windows. She always told him it was her dream car, and he wanted to make her feel extra special on her day. He was also trying hard to get back in her good graces. He noticed a major change in Bonnie but he thought it was because of his mess ups. Word hadn't got back to him about she and Karl but it was only a matter of time before Karl sent word.

That night, Bonnie prepared for a night out with the girls. She planned on celebrating with Monique and Tess, and then hooking up with Karl afterwards. Ted went home early under the impression he would be taking Bonnie out for her birthday like he did every year, but Bonnie wasn't feeling like the usual. When Ted walked in, Bonnie was sitting on the edge of the bed putting on a pair of fabulous Louboutins. She was wearing a royal blue dress from Neiman's that hugged her coca cola frame just right.

"You can't bowl in that," Ted said. *I know this nigga don't think I wanna go fucking bowling on my birthday*, Bonnie thought to herself.

"I'm going out with the girls," she said.

"Oh okay. That's wassup," he said, nonchalantly. "Where ya'll going?"

"Bleu Martini," she replied.

"Alright then. Have fun," he said, trying to hide his irritation. Bonnie sprayed on her Chance Chanel perfume, grabbed her keys and pocket book and headed out the door. Ted watched her through the window as she jumped into her Range Rover, and peeled off.

When Bonnie got to Bleu Martini her girls were already there waiting for her with a birthday cake and shots of Ciroc. "Happy Birthday girl!" Monique and Tess shouted. "Aww thanks you guys!" Bonnie replied. "I love you bitches!"

"We love you too, now c'mon bottoms up!" Monique shouted.

The three of them raised their glasses, and tossed the peach Ciroc down their throats. "Girl the way you movin' got me in a trance. DJ turn me up ladies this yo jam. Imma sip Moscato and you gon' loose them pants. And Imma throw this money while you do it with no hands…" Bonnie jumped up from the table, "This my shit!" Monique and Tess quickly followed. They went to the middle of the dance floor and stole everyone's attention immediately.

Bleu Martini was poppin' and they stayed turned up all night long. Monique and Tess invited their boyfriends and they brought out some real getting money players. The girls definitely created a husky tab and they didn't spend a dime of their money.

Meanwhile, Karl was at home waiting for Bonnie to come over. She told him she would only be a couple of hours, but she ended up staying until closing. By the time she made it to his spot it was three in the morning, and he was hot about it. When she called him to open the gate, he didn't even say a word to her. He just hung up in her ear, and buzzed her in.

"You all drunk and shit," he said, with a frown on his face.

"So what. It's my birthday," she said.

"Why would those bitches let you drive like this? You could've got into an accident."

"Hell, we were all drunk. Besides, I know how to handle the wheel when I'm drunk."

"You want a t-shirt or something to sleep in?"

"I can't stay Karl," she said. "I can only stay for an hour or so."

"I been waiting on you all fucking night. You ain't going nowhere."

Bonnie just stood there with a confused look on her face. What was she going to say…she couldn't tell him no.

Not Karl. She followed him into his bedroom, took her clothes off, changed into one of his white t-shirts and climbed into bed with him. Karl turned his back towards her and said he was going to sleep. But there was something about the way the words left his mouth that made Bonnie feel like something was wrong.

"Are you okay?" she asked.

"Yeah I'm good," he said, in a low voice. She moved closer to him and put her arms around him from behind.

"You bold as shit B," he said.

"Why do you say that?" she asked.

"Do you really have to ask why? You crossed me with my man, and now you crossing him by fucking back with me. I feel like a fucking nut for even dealing with you." Bonnie laid there bewildered by what he was saying. She didn't have a clue where all of this was coming from.

"Karl why are you bringing all of this up?"

"What you mean? Shit, it needs to be brought up. What you did was some whore shit! You crossed me in the worse way possible!" he said, raising his voice.

"You said you forgave me…I should've known better," she said.

"No, I should've fucking known better. What's so crazy is that you actually fell in love with this nigga. You was never supposed to start loving him B." He raised up and sat on the edge of the bed and continued scolding her.

"You should've used that nigga and took his bread and held me down while I was in the joint! You don't fucking turn your back on the one who loved you and took care of your muthafuckin ass!"

"It's time for me to go," she said. "Cause I see where this is headed."

"You ain't going nowhere Bonnie! Sit your ass down!" Bonnie did exactly what she was told. "How many times do I have to say I'm sorry?" she asked.

"You fucked us up Bonnie. You fucked us up bad…how are we supposed to move past this?"

As much as she didn't want to hear it, she knew every word he was saying was true. She thought about what everyone had been telling her time and time again…"It'll never work between you and Karl, he'll never truly forgive you." She buried her face in her hands and tears began flowing from her eyes. Seeing Bonnie cry stopped Karl dead in his tracks. He wrapped his arm around her, and started wiping her tears.

"You know I hate it when you cry," he said. "I'm sorry."

"You just don't understand. If I could go back and change things I would," she sobbed.

"I know B. Stop crying," he said, while holding her close to his chest.

It hurt Karl deeply that Bonnie left him and had a baby by Ted. He knew Bonnie always wanted to have a baby and he hated he wasn't able to give that to her. Deep down he knew if it wasn't for his foolish ways she would've never lost their baby. Remembering those days is what made Karl soften up when it came to Bonnie. Although her moves were as scandalous as it gets, he knew he caused Bonnie a lot of pain and suffering. And because of this, he couldn't stop loving her, nor could he let her go. They went from having a heated argument to making passionate love all night long. Their love was crazy like that and always had been.

They slept until twelve noon and Bonnie woke up to numerous missed calls from Ted. In her mind she was stressing about what the hell she was going to say to him. She'd never stayed out on him before and the fact that she didn't answer any of his calls made her all the more nervous. She tried to keep her cool in front of Karl though. She didn't want to panic and leave in a hurry, causing Karl to feel some kind of way about rushing home to Ted. But still, Ted was her man. The father of her son, and she felt terrible about blatantly disrespecting him in that way.

When Bonnie finally left Karl's apartment, she went to her father's house to get Sean. On the ride over she concocted a story to tell Ted. She waited until she got to her father's house before she called him. She thought it would look better if she called from Michael's home number. Just by the tone of his voice when he answered "hello," Bonnie knew he was furious with her. She explained to him she was so intoxicated she couldn't drive and she passed out at Monique's house. She told him she left her car parked in Old City over night. After listening to the lies Bonnie told, he made it very clear he knew she was full of shit. Ted was not one to scream and yell. No matter how angry he was, he would always remain cool, calm and collected. After Ted hung up in Bonnie's ear she felt as though she was being pulled in so many directions. She was stressed and overwhelmed by the whole situation. She was fooling herself, thinking she could creep with Karl without there being any conflict. It was just a feeling she got that day. There was something in the air that gave Bonnie the feeling that shit was about to hit the fan.

CHAPTER FIFTEEN
The Blame Game

Bonnie sat on the passenger side, while Karl drove through the bottom of West Philly. They were sitting in the house chilling until his phone rang and then suddenly he had to make a quick run. Karl hadn't been completely honest with Bonnie about leaving the drug game alone. He wanted to paint a picture for her that he was a changed man and he was only focused on establishing himself as an author and entrepreneur. Karl pulled up on the corner of 38th and Brooklyn St and became irritated when he realized his homeboy still wasn't there. "This pussy getting on my fuckin' nerves!" he yelled out, as he picked up his cell phone to call him.

"Smoke where the fuck you at?" Karl asked in annoyance. "I'm on the block!"

"I'm around the corner, pulling up in less than five," he said.

"Nigga hurry the fuck up, you got me out here with all this shit on me!" he said, referring to the thirty thousand in cash and bags of rock cocaine tucked in a secret compartment under the steering wheel.

"My bad player. I be right there!"

Bonnie looked at Karl out of the corner of her eyes with disgust. This entire scene was all too familiar to her. *Here we go again with this shit* she thought to herself. Bonnie had grown so much since the old days when riding dirty with Karl and hearing him check niggas actually turned her on. Now she was looking at him like he was a hot mess. It made her wonder what other bad habits still lingered.

When Smoke finally pulled up Karl hopped out of the car very aggressively and with a menacing scowl on his face. All Bonnie could hear was "nigga this and nigga that!" The corner was poppin' as usual and everybody was eyeing them as Karl pointed his finger and was scolding Smoke as if he was his son. Smoke stood about 6'5 and was very heavy set with a grimy, gutter look. You wouldn't think this beastly looking dude would allow another man to come at him in this way, especially in front of a crowd. Bonnie never did understand why everyone let Karl get away with talking to them so greasy. She knew one day his cut throat ways and failure to show respect to others would eventually catch up to him.

Ever since Bonnie started seeing Karl again, she was different with Ted. She stayed gone a lot and was distant, even when she was home. She would cop an attitude with him over the smallest things, just looking for a reason to leave him. But after a while she began to feel like she was making all the wrong moves. It seemed as though Karl's love for Bonnie would go in and out and his mood swings were giving her a bad case of whiplash.

She knew that Karl and Ted were in contact from time to time but Karl always told Bonnie that it was strictly about car business and so did Ted. It was weird because deep down inside Karl hated him but he'd mastered the art of keeping your friends close and your enemies closer. He kept a tint on his true feelings and pretended as though there was no love lost.

One Sunday morning, Ted, Bonnie and the baby were at Ihop eating breakfast when Karl called. Her heart dropped to the floor and just listening to them exchange words back and forth was nerve-racking. She felt like a piece of shit because

Ted was laughing and joking with him, all the while she was fucking Karl behind his back. Yes, Ted crossed Karl and stole Bonnie. Now Karl was trying to steal her back. Or was he? As much as he wanted to, Karl knew he could never be with Bonnie again. What would the streets say? They would call him weak, a nut, a pussy…and he could never go out like that. He cared too much about other people's perception of him. Now, fucking around with Bonnie was a different story. He wanted people to know that, especially since he was so embarrassed by what happened. Fucking around with her again made him feel like he'd won. But in a game with no rules, there are no winners.

It was a hot and rainy day, and Bonnie was just leaving L.A. Fitness on City Line Avenue. She was wearing a pair of grey tights, a cut off tank top and Nike sneakers. Her hair was pulled up in a messy bun, and her baby hair laid on the back of her neck and forehead. As she walked through the parking lot she was approached left and right by random dudes before she made it to her car. "Damn ma you bad as shit! Put my number in your phone!" Bonnie sucked her teeth, hit unlock on the remote and hopped into her Range Rover. "Damn these niggas be so thirsty," she said to herself in annoyance. Karl had been expecting her so she drove straight over to his apartment, which was only a few minutes away.

"Hey baby," Bonnie said. He hugged her, and then smacked her ass. "That thang fat as shit!" he said, and Bonnie just smiled.

"So what did you want to talk to me about?" Bonnie asked.

"I just wanted to look you in your face and tell you how much I appreciate you."

"You do?" she asked, with a big smile on her face.

"Yo, the way you just stepped in and helped me with that book shit! I love you for that shit B!" he said, excitedly. "I always admired how you handle business."

"Thanks baby," she said.

"Together we the shit. With you by my side it's nothing I

can't accomplish," he said. "You make my life better."

Bonnie played a major part in the editing process of his new book and made sure that everything was formatted properly. She even made phone calls back and forth to the printing company whenever Karl was unhappy with something. She took a lot of pressure off of him and did whatever he needed her to do. When he released the book it did very well on the streets. He didn't have a major publishing company behind him or anything like that. It was just him doing all the grinding. And Karl was a hustler at heart so pushing books was nothing to him. Hell, he could sell water to a whale.

In Karl's eyes, he and Bonnie were like Jay Z and Beyonce. She was that chick he believed could compliment any deal. He really believed they could be on some boss shit and conquer the world together. Only problem was, she had a baby by his mans. It always came back down to that. No matter how good things were between them, how good she made him feel or how hard she tried to please him; her past mistakes would always resurface.

At this point, Bonnie had enough of Karl loving her one day and then hating her the next. He told Bonnie that the only way they had any chance at a future together was if they moved out of state. He even had the audacity to tell her to prove to him that she was serious by moving first and once she was settled, then he would follow. She loved him whole heartedly but she wasn't going to deal with him on those terms. She would rather let him go than to play his game. Bonnie cursed him out, told him to lose her number and then hung up in his ear. She called T-mobile and told them that she needed a number change. She knew that Karl would be calling her and she wanted to make him feel like shit after hearing the operator say, "The number you reached is not in service." And just like she expected Karl tried calling her that night. He wasn't sure if she changed her number or if she just needed to pay her bill. So, he messaged her on Facebook.

The next morning, Bonnie saw the message notification

on her cell phone from Karl and this put a huge smile on her face. "I knew I would make that nigga sick!" she said, giggling to herself. "He got me fucked up," she said out loud while dialing *67 before his number. Karl anxiously picked up on the first ring.

"Hello," he answered.

"Yeah. What's up?"

"Why the fuck you calling me from a blocked number?" he asked.

"Because you don't know how to act. That's why," Bonnie said, in a nonchalant tone.

"B I'm sorry I been trippin', but c'mon put yourself in my shoes."

"Karl that shit is getting old. We keep going back to the same thing, so just leave me the fuck alone! I'm over this shit!" Bonnie said, raising her voice.

"Yo calm down," he said. "Unblock your number and call me back."

"Naw I'm cool," she said. "I'ma stay where I'm at and make my situation work."

"Bitch you better watch how the fuck you talking to me!"

"Fuck you Karl. I'm not putting up with your shit…I'm out!" she said.

Bonnie was just trying to give him a reality check, she wasn't really done with him, but Karl took all of her words to heart and he was flaming inside. When Bonnie told him that she was going to make her situation work, it made him furious. He wasn't going to lose to Ted a second time around. Oh hell no, he wasn't having that. Karl wouldn't be satisfied until he broke them up for good. It was time to hit Ted where it would hurt.

"T what's up?"

"What's up Karl?"

"Just calling to warn you about your bitch. That bitch ain't cool!" he said, in a hateful tone.

Although the words, "What bitch?" left Ted's mouth, he

knew exactly who Karl was referring to. His heart dropped to his feet. It was like that jail call all over again, when he and Karl had a screaming match about Bonnie a couple years back.

"B! That bitch out of pocket dog. She…"

"Watch your mouth dog she ain't no bitch, that's my baby mom," Ted interrupted.

"Well your baby mom been on my dick since the time I came home."

"And nigga you just now telling me this shit?"

"Cause I'm tired of playing with her muthafuckin' ass! I don't want shit else to do with her. And I'm just calling to let you know your circle ain't tight. She told me she ain't feeling you no more and all that. Hell, she was ready to move with me and everything."

Ted just held the phone in complete silence while Karl ranted on. He wanted to hear everything that Karl had to say.

"Nigga I could've took her and your son away from you. But I ain't into that. I'm not gon' do you how you did me."

"You been around my son?" Ted asked, raising his voice.

"Yeah lots of times," Karl said lying through his teeth. She at my house a couple times a week and all that. Yo I'm just letting you know that you need to tighten up your circle. She ain't no good for you. She's a good girl gone bad." Karl said.

"Did you fuck her?" Ted asked.

Karl was no fool. He knew that if he would have told Ted the truth then that would be his ass. He would be just as guilty as Bonnie and he knew that Ted would never fuck with him again. Furthermore, he knew Bonnie was the type of woman that a muthafucka would kill for and Ted could easily pay someone to get rid of Karl for good. So he played it smart. He lied.

"Man hell naw I ain't fuck her! I wouldn't touch her with a ten foot pole," he said. "Especially after she crossed me with you!"

"So then why you so mad nigga? What the fuck is this

really all about?" Ted spat.

"Nigga it's about you and me! You wasn't supposed to ever love her! She was my bitch T. She still my bitch, you just had a baby by her!" All of Karl's true feelings were being exposed now. Since, the day he came home he'd been pretending to honor the *bros before hoes* code but truthfully he was sick about it. And he had enough of the fake shit. He knew this day was coming and it was quite refreshing to let it all out.

"She'll do anything I tell her to! I could make her go strip if I needed her to! I taught her ass everything she know. Shit, I fucking made her who the fuck she is today!"

The silence on the other end of the phone is the only thing that stopped Karl's rant.

"Hello?" Karl said, checking to see if Ted was still there.

"Look dog, at the end of the day she was your girl first. If she choose you this time around then so be it. It is what it is," Ted said, in a nonchalant tone. He swerved around in his big Escalade truck, making an illegal U-turn so that he could get back on Hwy 76. His blood was boiling and he couldn't wait to confront Bonnie, but all the while he was fronting to Karl like he could care less.

"Whatever ya'll do that's on ya'll. I don't give a fuck," Ted said.

"Well just tell her to stop calling my muthafuckin phone from blocked numbers and shit, I'm done with her ass," Karl replied.

"Thanks for the call, good looking out," he said, with a smirk on his face.

"You was my man T, you should've never let a bitch come between us nigga. And you still my man. That's the only reason why I'm calling you with this," Karl said, manipulatively.

Ted knew that was bullshit. Karl was trying to kick it as though he was looking out for him. But Ted knew this was only the get back.

"Alright my nigga. I'm out. I'll holler at you," Ted said,

and then hung up the phone.

What was usually a forty-five minute ride from South Philly to Bucks County, where he and Bonnie lived only took twenty minutes that day. He was livid, and at that moment he believed he was done with Bonnie.

Bonnie was upstairs folding laundry when Ted came in and slammed the door. Sean was sitting on the floor playing with his toys. The slamming of the door startled the both of them. As Bonnie approached the staircase, she saw Ted coming up the stairs fast paced, and with an unpleasant expression on his face.

"What's wrong baby?" Bonnie asked.

"I should've known better than to fuck with you!" he spat. "Out of all the niggas in the city you been fucking with Karl?"

"What are you talking about?"

"Don't act like you don't know what the fuck I'm talking about! He called me and told me everything!"

"All I did was help him with his book, that's all," she said.

"You shouldn't of been talking to him at all Bonnie. This whole time you let this nigga smile in my face while you been fucking around with him Bonnie!"

"It wasn't like that Ted. I swear." The tears began to fall from Bonnie's eyes. She felt like the world was caving in on her. She never would've thought Karl would stoop this low. *What kind of nigga would do some shit like this*, she thought to herself.

"You crossed me! You been in this nigga house? You had my muthafuckin son around that nigga?"

'He's lying. I never took Sean around him. Ever! I would never do that!" she said, still crying.

"You can cry me a fucking river I don't give a fuck. I'm done with you!" he said. "You been calling this nigga all hours of the night and shit."

"So, you're just going to believe everything he told you?"

"Yup cause you had no business fucking with him in the

first place. You made me look like a nut Bonnie."

"After everything you took me through Ted, I can't believe you're so quick to walk away from me because of this."

"So what I'm a man. You never hurt a man's pride. It could've been any other nigga but him. That was the most slimy shit you could've ever done."

"I'm sorry but you haven't been treating me right either. You've been taking me for granted."

"I'm not trying to hear that shit. You told him you wanted to move with him to Atlanta? I would be a fool to stay with you Bonnie."

"This is exactly what he wants. I was done with him. That's why I changed my number. He got mad and sent me messages on Facebook, I'll show them to you."

Bonnie grabbed her cell phone, pulled up Karl's Facebook messages and then handed Ted the phone.

"See, it's all right there. That's the only reason he called you. I was never going to leave you for him and he knew that. He would've never called you if I didn't change my number."

"Still, why would you even deal with him? This is the same nigga that used to beat on you and treat you like shit."

"You don't understand. There was never any closure between us," she said. "I left him for you while he was in jail Ted."

"Well you should've stayed with him then. I blame myself. I should've known better," he said, while grabbing his car keys.

"Where are you going?" Bonnie asked.

"Don't worry about it," Ted said, his voice as cold as ice.

Bonnie grabbed his arm and pleaded for him to stay. He yanked his arm away from her, stormed downstairs and left out the door. Bonnie could hear his tires screeching as he sped out of the driveway. All she could do was cry. She felt so stupid. How did she get herself into such a mess? At times she could be her own worst enemy. "I can't stand him! I hate him!" Bonnie said out loud to herself, as she dialed Karl's number.

"Yo," he answered.

"I can't believe you Karl. How could you do this to me?" Bonnie sobbed.

"I told you to stop playing with me. You shouldn't have changed your number on me."

"So you've been lying to me all this time? Was it all a game to you?"

"This ain't about you Bonnie. This was a lesson for him. He should've never crossed me the way he did. He wasn't supposed to fall in love with you. And I told him that."

"You hurt me once again Karl. All you did was use me to get your revenge."

"If I wanted to hurt you I would've told him we fucked. Like I said, It wasn't about you."

"Well I'm hurting bad right now. And it's all because of you."

"I didn't mean to hurt you B. And I don't want us to be over. I still need you in my life. I'm gon' still need your help with a lot of shit, especially the book."

"You got a lot of fucking nerve. Why would I want to help you after what you just did to me? I'm done with you! It's over for good this time!" she said, and then hung up in his ear.

Bonnie was distraught. She just laid across her bed and let the tears flow onto her pillow. In her head, she could hear Tess and Monique's voices telling her not to trust Karl and he was only out for revenge. She thought about everything she'd been through over the past few years. All of the bad choices and wrong turns she made. Thinking back to when she and Karl were together and how she ended up with Ted made her feel like she was responsible for all the pain she felt today. What goes around sure does come back around again. And Karma was staring Bonnie straight in the face.

Later that night, Ted and Bonnie talked when he came home. He had some time to cool off and evaluate the entire situation. Although, he was still upset about what she'd done, he realized Karl was only trying to break them up. He knew Karl was still in love with Bonnie. It was obvious in the things he said. Ted could hear the hurt and anger in his voice. He could see Karl still loved Bonnie.

Ted told her he was willing to work it out. He admitted he stopped appreciating her and that he took her love for granted. He also revealed to Bonnie her going back to Karl was a fear of his, which is why he kept his guard up. Ted looked Bonnie square in the eyes and said, "At least you didn't fuck him. Shit I would've left you for that." She just stared at him and thought to herself *If only you knew*. He told Bonnie they were going to get through it and from this day forward they were starting over with a clean slate.

A few days later Bonnie woke up to a long message from Karl on Facebook. He made sure he changed his profile picture to one that he thought would make her sick. In the picture he had his arms wrapped around a brown skinned woman, and she was smiling as if she was so happy to be with him. His message read…

Bonnie I hope you're doing okay. I want you to know I never meant to hurt you. I also pray you forgive me for everything I've ever done to you because I have forgiven you. What happened between us does not define who you are. I want you to continue to do great things with your life and keep smiling because you are beautiful inside and out. I've moved on with someone who really loves me and who I've grown to love. I'm getting married next week and I'm leaving everything and everybody else alone. Take care. This is closure.

All Bonnie could do was shake her head after reading his message. She knew damn well he hadn't moved on that fast. She was used to him jumping from one chick to another, so it didn't faze her one bit. Bonnie knew whoever the broad was, she was only temporary.

Over the next few months, Bonnie stayed away from Karl. She thought about him a lot and there was no denying she still loved him. But what was she going to do? She finally accepted they could never be. It was clear every road was a dead end street. And as much as it hurt she had to live with the choices she made. It wasn't as if she didn't love Ted or that she wasn't content with their relationship. She loved her son more than anything else and she decided she would make her family work. The funny thing is, what happened actually brought them closer together. It made their bond stronger and also taught them to appreciate one another.

Bonnie's favorite cousin Delilah, from Atlanta was getting married. Bonnie flew in the day before so she could help her girl with any last minute preparations. She and Delilah shared a close bond since they were kids, so it made sense for Bonnie to be her matron of honor. For some reason, during the wedding all she could think about was Karl. After the reception and way too many drinks, she gave him a call.

When *private call* flashed across his cell phone screen he smiled from the ear to ear. Bonnie was the only one that called him from blocked numbers, so he anxiously answered on the first ring.

"Hello."

"Hey Karl."

"What's up Bonnie?"

"Nothing. Just calling to see how you were doing."

"I'm good B. What about yourself?"

"I'm okay."

"You coming to my book signing?"

"Yup. If you want me to," she said in a soft tone. "Can I ask you a question?"

"Yeah. What's up?"

"Do you still love me?" she asked.

"I still love you. It's impossible for me to stop loving you B."

"Wow," she said. "I feel the same way."

"Yo, you wanna know something crazy?"

"What?"

"I just met this girl that look just like you. She act like you, talk like you and everything."

"I doubt that," she said.

"You want me to send you a picture of her?"

"Fuck no. I don't need to see her," she said, in her most irritated voice.

"I finally found someone that can give me what you gave me B."

"Oh boy here we go again. Let's see how long this last," she said.

"No it's different this time. She's the only one that has my attention right now."

"Well I'm happy for you Karl. I gotta go," she said. Bonnie hung up the phone, wondering who the hell this new girl was. Who was he so excited about?

The girl's name was Cassie Cummings. She was only eighteen years old, and fresh out of high school. They met at Yummy's Diner in West Philly. She was on her way in and he was on his way out, and there was just something about her face that reminded him of Bonnie instantly. Maybe it was the almond shaped eyes, those full pink lips, or her curvaceous body. Whatever it was, she stopped Karl dead in his tracks. They exchanged numbers and from that day forward they were inseparable.

Bonnie waited a few weeks before she called Karl again. She was hoping he was on to the next and not still with this Cassie chick. She could handle him jumping from one chick to another but the thought of him actually taking someone serious drove her crazy. She asked him how he was doing and the first thing that came out of his mouth was that he was expecting a baby.

"With who? The girl you were telling me about?"

"Yup."

"Damn you just met her. Now she's pregnant?" Bonnie asked, sarcastically.

"Yeah," he replied.

"Wow," she said. "Are you happy?"

"Yeah, I'm happy. I need something to keep me focused out here."

"Well, I'm happy for you Karl," she said, trying to hide

the hurt.

"Thank you," he said. "I just hope it's real this time."

Bonnie knew he was referring to what happened to their love and how it was so easily destroyed. Now he was moving on with someone else and about to have a baby. It hurt Bonnie to her heart. She believed Karl was only doing this to even the score. And she was right. Karl wasn't in love with this new girl but he loved the fact she reminded him so much of Bonnie. It felt like he was getting a second chance at making things right between him and her. So he didn't move slow. Karl moved Cassie into his apartment and took very good care of her. He spoiled her and gave her anything she wanted. When she hit her fourth month of pregnancy, Karl surprised her with a classic Harry Winston emerald-cut engagement ring.

A week later, they went to the courthouse and got married. He made sure he broadcasted it all over the social networks so that word would get back to Bonnie. He posted pictures of the two of them leaving the courthouse, with the caption "me and my new wife." It hurt Bonnie to the core but it's what she needed. She needed to know he seriously moved on with someone else. She would never be able to let him go but she was able to let go of the idea that they would find their way back to each other. For some odd reason, this gave her closure and peace of mind. She was finally over all the should've, would've could've thoughts and accepting things for what they were. But just when she was feeling like everything was going to be alright tragedy hit full force…one that would change her life forever.

It was August 14, 2012, and Bonnie was out with Monique and Tess. While at the club, she received a text from Karl's daughter that she'd been trying to reach her. Bonnie's cell phone wasn't receiving a good signal so a lot of her calls weren't getting through. Bonnie was drinking and partying so hard, she said to herself *I'll just call her in the morning…I'm sure it's nothing that can't wait until tomorrow.*

That following morning, Bonnie woke up with a

hangover. She dragged herself out of bed and went straight to the medicine cabinet for some Advil. She called Sierra but didn't get an answer. She logged onto Instagram and as she was scrolling through her news feed she saw pictures of Karl posted by numerous people, with the caption R.I.P. She clicked on Sierra's page and there it was…R.I.P. Dad I love you. Bonnie couldn't believe her eyes. She texted Sierra and she confirmed her father was shot eleven times and four times in the head.

Bonnie could hardly breathe and she could feel a huge knot growing in her stomach. She felt like someone stabbed her with a knife. She hadn't talked to him in months but the night before he messaged her on Facebook out of the clear blue. He asked her if she was alright. She wrote back *Yes, thanks for asking. How about you?* And she never got a response from him. She got out of bed and walked into the bathroom where Ted was brushing his teeth. Why she was running to him, she didn't know.

"Karl got killed," she said. Ted was unsure if she was asking him or telling him.

"He did?" he asked. "What happened?"

"He was shot," she said, in a low voice. "I can't believe this," she said, as she put both hands on her head.

"Damn that's fucked up," he said.

"I know. I just can't believe it," she said, turning her back towards him. Tears welled up in her eyes and the pit of her stomach began to ache. She placed her hand over mouth and let out a cry, that she was trying so hard to hold in.

Bonnie walked out of the bathroom, wanting to get out of the house as quickly as possible. She needed to cry, she needed to let it all out but she was afraid to show all her emotions in front of Ted. What would he think? How would he feel seeing her so distraught over Karl's death? Bonnie quickly dressed Sean and herself. She slipped on a pair of leggings, a t-shirt and put a Chanel hat on her head. The moment she got into the car and drove off the tears started flowing. She was crying so hard she couldn't see clearly.

"I thought that things like this get better with time, but I still need you. Why is that? You're the only image in my mind so I still see you around. I miss you like every day. I want to be with you but you're away..." Beyonce's "I miss you" was playing on the radio and she just lost it. She turned the radio off but that didn't stop the deep pain. She dropped Sean off at her father's and then drove to Tess's house. She'd been calling Monique nonstop but didn't get an answer. It seemed on that particular morning she couldn't get any of her family or friends on the phone.

"Hey Sierra."

"Hey Bonnie."

"How are you feeling?"

"Not good. I still can't believe it. I just keep praying that he'll just wake up."

"Wait. What do you mean wake up? Where is he?"

"He's at Penn, in intensive care."

"I'm on my way there now," she said, anxiously, as she pushed down harder on the gas pedal. "What happened last night? He messaged me around nine."

"He was at a cookout in West Philly, and somebody shot him eleven times," she said. "It happened around ten-thirty. *Wow* Bonnie thought to herself. *Maybe he knew something was going to happen. Is that why he reached out to me last night? Damn Karl who did this to you?*

"And nobody knows who did it? Nobody's talking?" Bonnie asked.

"Nope don't nobody know nothing," she said. "But you know my dad had a lot of enemies, it could've been anybody.

"That's true. But somebody knows something, trust me. It's only a matter of time before it comes out," Bonnie said. "Where were his friends when this happened?"

"They were there but they said it happened when my dad was walking to his car."

"That's crazy. Well I'm on my way to the hospital, I'll call you later."

"Okay love you."

"Love you too."

Bonnie's eyes were blood shot red by the time she arrived at Tess's house. Tess couldn't believe it when she told her what happened to Karl. She got dressed in a hurry and jumped into the driver's side of Bonnie's Range Rover, so she could get her best friend to the hospital. Bonnie sat on the passenger side with a blank face and in a daze. All she could do was think about everything they'd been through over the years. She couldn't believe this was happening.

When Bonnie got to the hospital she didn't know what to expect. She thought Karl's new wife Cassie would be there by his side and she didn't know how she would react but one thing for sure…she wasn't going to let anyone stop her from seeing him.

When Bonnie got to the front desk the receptionist told her repeatedly, they didn't have a Karl Atkins in the system. She called Karl's mother to confirm he was at Penn Hospital. Ms. Lynn told Bonnie yes and that they've been telling everyone they didn't have him there.

Bonnie told the receptionist he was in the intensive care unit and to check for anyone brought in critical condition around eleven o' clock. "Here he is, Room 5021. I couldn't find him because he's in the system as unknown," she said. The receptionist advised Bonnie to get in touch with someone who could provide the hospital with proper identification and then they could have him listed. Bonnie called his mother and told her she was on her way up to see him and she would have to bring his driver's license. His mother said, "I knew if anyone was going to get in to see Karl, it would be you." "Of course," Bonnie replied.

Walking into that room and seeing Karl lying there by himself had really set Bonnie off. She didn't understand how he could've been listed in the system as unknown in the first place. Wasn't his wife supposed to handle that? And where was she? Karl always hated being alone, and there he was lying in a hospital bed without a person in sight. He was hooked up to a ventilator machine and his head was wrapped in bandages, that were stained in blood. His chest was moving up and down, and Bonnie placed her hand over his heart and she could feel it still beating. It looked as though he was only sleeping. Bonnie stood over him, holding his hand and crying, "Karl it's me Bonnie. I'm here," she said. "Can you hear me?"

"Excuse me are you two family?" A blonde haired nurse asked.

"I'm his ex-wife," Bonnie responded.

"Okay. I'll leave you guys alone," she said.

Bonnie pulled up a chair and sat next to him, still holding his hand. *I wonder if he knows I'm here*, she thought to herself. "Guess what your mom said, she said that if anyone was going to get in here to see you, she knew it would be me." Bonnie laughed out loud to herself, with tears rolling down her cheeks. "See baby, everyone knows I don't play when it comes to you." Suddenly the rhythm of the vital sign monitor's beeping changed. Bonnie got excited because she believed that Karl could hear every word that she was saying.

As soon as the nurse walked in, Bonnie started bombarding her with a ton of questions. "Why is the machine beeping like that? Does this mean he can hear me? Is he trying to respond?" she quizzed.

"No, I'm sorry sweetie. Sometimes the machine just does that, it has nothing to do with him at all," she said.

"Do you think he'll come out of this?"

"I don't. His injuries were too severe. He's been declared brain dead," she said. "I'm sorry."

"But how can he be brain dead, when his heart is still beating? I mean…Look at him, he's sweating and everything."

"His heart continues to beat because it's artificially being supplied oxygen from the ventilator. His heart will only continue to beat for a short amount of time. In most cases two to three days," the nurse said, in a sympathetic voice.

Bonnie couldn't get a single word out after hearing that.

She buried her face in her hands and just cried. The nurse patted her on the shoulder before leaving out of the room. "I still don't believe he can't hear me Tess. I don't care what they say," she sobbed. Tess hugged Bonnie real tight and said, "Of course he can B. He knows you're here."

Bonnie spent the entire day at the hospital with Karl. She would've stayed the night if she could have, but it wasn't her place. When she got home that night Ted tried so hard to read her. He wanted to know how she was feeling, and if she was effected by Karl's death at all. She went to bed without saying a single word to him. He could clearly see she was hurting, and he was pissed off about it.

Over the next few days, Bonnie was sick. She couldn't eat, sleep or even think straight. All she could do was think about Karl and what they once shared. Whenever she closed her eyes, she still saw his face. There was no escaping it. The more she thought about everything, the more guilty and regretful she felt. She believed she was partly responsible for all of this. Karl always told her she ruined his life and all of their plans. When Karl got out of prison, they were supposed leave Philly and start a new life together. *Damn. Why didn't I wait for you Karl? I should've just held on a little tighter. None of this would have happened*, she thought to herself.

Bonnie received a call from Karl's daughter informing her they were taking Karl off of life support later that day. That's when it really hit her. Karl was gone and he wasn't coming back. There would be no more of the back and forth games between the two of them. No more calling him in the middle of the night just to hear his voice. It was officially over.

She went to the hospital to say one last and final goodbye. When Bonnie got there a woman was standing next to his bed in tears, telling him she was going to miss him. When Bonnie walked in, the woman stepped back not knowing if she was the wife or not. She said goodbye and then left Bonnie alone with him.

"Hey baby, it's me again. I guess I'm supposed to say

goodbye. But I can't. I know I'll see you again. I love you."
She kissed him on the lips and then on the forehead, the way
he always used to kiss her. She grabbed the letter out of her
pocket that she wrote for him. She folded the letter and then
placed it in the pocket of his hospital gown. The letter read...

*Karl I'm still in shock and I can't believe what's happening right
now. I want you to know that I love you, I always have. You will forever
be the love of my life. I know we've been through a lot together, some good
and some bad but I don't regret any of it. You've taught me so much and
made me the woman I am today. Thank you for that. Just know I'll
never stop loving you. Yours Always, B.*

Bonnie didn't stay long. She didn't want to be there
when everyone else arrived, but Sierra texted her throughout
everything keeping her updated. Karl passed away only two
minutes after pulling the plug. Bonnie asked Sierra if his wife
or anyone else found the letter she left in his pocket, and she
said no. That didn't make sense to her. How did his wife not
find it? *If she's grieving the way I am then she would have found it*, she
thought. Their whole marriage was nothing more than a joke
to Bonnie. She didn't take it serious not one bit. She knew he
was only with Cassie because she reminded him of her. And
all of his friends and family knew as well.

The funeral was held two days later, on a Friday. Out of
all the days, it just had to be pouring down raining. Bonnie
was dressed in all black and wore her hair pulled to the back
in a ponytail. Bonnie, Tess and Monique all sat in the second
row behind his immediate family. His wife, who didn't cry the
entire service, sat next to his mother with a blank expression
on her face. Bonnie didn't even have the strength to view the
body. The church was so packed people were lined up against
the walls. She didn't know who was there and she didn't want
anything getting back to Ted about her breaking down at
Karl's funeral. So she remained seated and hid her teary eyes
behind a huge pair of Gucci shades.

At the burial there was a lot of breaking down and Karl's
chicks were coming out of the woodwork. Bonnie seen many
familiar faces, especially those she had beef with over Karl.

She even locked eyes with Michelle and after all the years that passed, she still wanted to whoop her ass just one more time. She and Michelle had a beef that would never die.

Bonnie went straight home after the funeral. She turned the television on and climbed into bed. Sean was at her father's for the day and she was looking forward to having some time to herself. But lying in bed all alone, only made her think of Karl even more. And then the tears started to fall again. She began talking out loud to herself, "It hurts so bad. It hurts so fucking bad." Suddenly, Bonnie heard the downstairs door shut. *Oh shit, I can't let him see me like this.* She jumped out of bed and ran into the bathroom. She wiped her tears but her eyes were still blood shot red.

Knock Knock Knock Knock "Yo, why you got the door locked?" he asked. Open the door."

"Huh?" she asked, stalling for time.

"What you doing? Open the door." She opened the door and tried to quickly walk out so that he wouldn't notice that she'd been crying.

"What you been crying?" he asked.

"A little," she said.

"You look like you been doing a whole lot of fucking crying," he said. "You that bothered about what happened to him?"

"You can't be serious. Of course I'm bothered by it," she said.

"You must still love the nigga then. I don't understand how he can whoop your ass and treat you like shit but yet you still love him. He didn't give a fuck about you." Ted said, in an angry tone.

"You can't tell me that he didn't love me, because I know he did," she said. "And why are you being so hateful. He was your friend at one point."

"Man if the tables were reversed he wouldn't give a fuck if I got killed," he said. "Shit if anything, it'll make him sleep better at night."

"Yeah cause you can sleep better at night right? You

don't have to worry about me and him anymore. Right?"

"I was never worried about him. He wasn't no threat to me," he said, lying. But Bonnie knew Karl being gone gave him a sense of relief and comfort.

"Well I can't pretend anymore I'm not hurt. Yes I'm hurt Ted. What the hell do you want me to do?"

"I don't want you to do shit. That's on your ass. I don't give a fuck," he said, as he left out of the bathroom. "If you knew he loved you so much then you should've stayed with him."

"Well it's too late for that isn't it?" she yelled down the hall, as Ted walked away.

Bonnie felt conflicted inside. She didn't know how she was going to make things right again but she knew she would have to make a drastic change. Being in Philly just didn't feel right anymore. She wanted to go somewhere and start fresh. She didn't want the constant reminder of a hurtful past. And in order for her to fully heal and move on she would have to leave Ted as well. In her heart she believed nothing positive could come of their relationship because it stemmed from something so negative. On the flip side, she was thankful for her son and also for all of the lessons she learned. But who would've thought it would play out like this? Life is a gamble, we're all players in the game...but those that roll the dice must be able to stand the sacrifice.

A Note from the Author

In life, we all make mistakes but the most important thing is that we learn from them. Unlike a game of chess, once you make a move it can't be undone. The choices and decisions you make, will shape your life forever.

ABOUT THE AUTHOR

Beverly Sade is a model and author from Philadelphia, Pa. The daughter of a screen writer and film producer, she learned at an early age that writing was her passion. She would write short stories and poetry. Beverly has received an editor's choice award for outstanding achievement in poetry, presented by The International Library of Poetry. She's been a featured model in some of the hottest videos, magazines and calendars. This is her second novel, Shadow of a Gold Digger was her debut.